THE SHYWATER SLEW

~

The Shywater Slew

A Novel

~

KYLE ZIMMERMAN

ZAM! Books
Atlanta, GA

Zam! Books
336640 Georgia Tech Station
Atlanta, GA 30332

ISBN-13: 978-0-6151-5161-8

First Zam! Books Paperback edition July 2007

10 9 8 7 6 5 4 3 2 1

Zam! Books is a trademark of Kyle Zimmerman

Printing by **Lulu, Inc.**

Designed by Kyle Zimmerman

For my parents,
Who always pushed knowledge above all else.

A man who is contented with what he has done will never be famous for what he will do.

To the reader,

I started writing this book in January of 2007. I wrote it on my laptop in my dorm at Georgia Institute of Technology in Atlanta, GA. Since I could remember, I was good at math and science and followed a college career in the same. Also since I could remember, writing was my way of saying things that could not be spoken.

In math, a number is a number regardless of how ever much you want it to be a word. A number can be a symbol, can be a range, and can be an answer to a significant problem, but it ends there. Words are slightly different.

Words can tell us of how people feel and look and smell and think. Words can lead us away from our laptops and dorm rooms and numbers.

I decided to write a book about a younger man named Frank. While I did have a friend in college named Frank, he is not my main character. The real Frank dropped out of school after three semesters. The made-up Frank is, well, made-up. In fact, everybody and every action in this book are simply a part of my imagination and my storytelling. I left the places to be real, because it is hard for people to understand made-up places.

As I began writing this book, I put similar qualities of people I knew into my characters. Honestly, the only reason I did this was because it was easier to write about. I found that the closer I had experienced a situation, the better I could detail it. While some of the situations in this book are slightly familiar to me, the majority of the book is a result of my dreams.

Much like the main character, Frank, I can get lost for hours daydreaming. The daydreams I have are a result of a subconscious I can't control and the actions I can. In January of 2007, I began to record this combination into written form, hence creating my novel.

After a month of writing, my daydreams seemed to be about my book and my book seemed to be about my daydreams. It became hard to find the reality in writing and I often would wake up in the middle of the night wondering if I had dreamt something or if I had written it. Frank's life and my life slowly merged into a solid imaginary state that could not be physically reached. The thoughts I had on the train in the morning were his too. The time I spent outside looking at the spring flowers were his too. And so the novel became its own identity.

There is nothing more in life I want than to be completely free and content in my thoughts. This novel is very close to that feeling.

Kyle Zimmerman

1

I always wished I was a superhero, or at least had a cool name like one. The Flash, The Green Lantern, Martin Luther King Jr. They had cool names *and* superpowers. I had neither. I was Frank, or should I say, am Frank. My name may tell you that I am brief and to the point. I am neither of these and instead often get lost in simple daydreaming.

At the end of this book I will save the world.

My friend's name is Tom Long and he is frank, no less. He's got black straggles of hair unevenly mopped on top of his head and warm, pink cheeks. His messy clothes match his messy body as he flops around life almost like an old, dirty mattress. When I told him I was going to write a novel he said, "I think it would be a *novel* idea to write a novel," and then he snickered to himself for a few seconds. I don't like when Tom makes stupid jokes. He also told me that it wasn't a good idea to put the ending of the story at the beginning.

"Frank, no one will want to read anymore of it if they already know the ending," Tom told me. I kept the end at the beginning because I don't like when Tom makes stupid jokes.

When I told Tom about my novel, we were in a car heading south down Interstate 95 towards our favorite Chinese restaurant. We were going with Tom's two friends, Gina and some girl whose name rhymed with Tambourine or close to it. Gina was a plump girl with a shirt on that she thought was good looking and I thought was just about half the size it needed to be. I didn't tell her that. The other girl had a nose ring and a henna tattoo of a scorpion. Gina drove us in her 1994 Chevy Cavalier and she always told us it was "the best value in America". I thought it was a piece of crap. It smelled like my Grandma's house and fabric softener combined, but it had a CD player, so she bought it. If the car was given to her for free, with season tickets to Magic Kingdom, and a full tank of gas, it still would not be the best value in America. The other girl was in the passenger seat in front of me and held up a CD for Gina's approval. Gina nodded her head and slipped it into the dash. When the music started playing the other girl turned to no one in particular and said, "Andrew Baker is so hot. His lyrics are eclectic. I think you'll like this song."

I hate any music that has a drum track.

Andrew Baker's song had a drum track. "He looks like Jesus and I love him," rattled the Tambourine. Gina giggled in agreement and they started bopping and singing poorly like many young girls do. Tom asked me about my novel.

"So what's it going to be about," said Tom.

"Raisins," I said.

"Raisins? What are you talking about?" Tom didn't like my idea of writing a novel about raisins. "You will never be able to write a good novel with the end at the beginning and both the end and the beginning are about raisins."

2

There I was again, in the corner of a hip, swinging college party in the Art District of our nation's capitol, picking out the raisins from a bowl of organic trail mix. Raisins were the only thing I liked about that trail mix. I could relate to raisins. Think about it. All the other snacks were at their prime. Nuts, apricots, pretzels, pineapple, ginger. They were all the best they could possibly taste. Not the raisins though. They used to be great. They used to be grapes. Everyone in the fruit world said, "To hell with grapes. If they can't stay ripe, they can't be fruit." Then the snack world gave them one more chance; one more chance to save their dignity before they shriveled up and died. So here they were, not only surviving, but they were the life-blood of the snacks. They were making something out of nothing. I was a raisin.

I thought that story was clever enough for a pick-up line a few minutes ago. It wasn't, so now I continue to eat more raisins.

Like I said, I am going to save the world at the end of this book. And since I haven't saved the world yet, that means you are reading as fast as I am writing. *How am I going to save the world?* What a silly question to ask. I definitely won't tell you that yet. But I know. *How do I know?* Ah, now that is where my story begins. You see, I have dreams that, one way or another, come true. No, really. That is why I am so confident in the end to my story. It all started about, er, six years ago. I was just about to turn sixteen when it happened.

Outside of a plain yellow house in Alexandria, VA, the large oak trees were scared stiff against another blast of cold wind. With no leaves to blanket them from the snow, the trees looked like awkward teenagers trying to find warmth at a midnight bus stop. It was by far the coldest winter in years. December 22nd was the day.

Inside, staring over the iced turf and rooftops was another awkward teenager. That was me. I was reading an old comic book. In this particular episode, the main character was a heroine with the power to see through any material from any distance away. She had just spotted a man in a dark jacket concealing a 28 mm revolver, a fake driver's license, and a curiously strong pack of mints. She didn't know they were strong, she could just assume.

A gust of wind smacked my window and I looked out at my neighbor's house all decorated for Christmas.

The next pages of the comic began to explain the heroine's plan of disarming the culprit, gathering a sea of police officers, and freshening her breath before anyone uncovered her true identity. It was stupendous.

I heard the garage door opening and looked again out my window to just miss my dad's Lincoln SUV pulling in. I closed the book and returned it to the depths of my closet. I actually didn't read many comic books anymore. I just stumbled over this one when I was trying to clean out my infamous closet (a mass so thick not even my heroine could see through).

As I rushed down stairs I heard my father speaking to the empty house as an audience. "Boy, looks like Mother Nature is in menopause because it is brutal out there".

I could almost here the drummer muster a *bah-duh splash.*

At dinner we discussed the usual. My hairy-faced father asked me what lazy activities I came up with again on this "Holiday Break". My mother was too busy sneaking extra broccoli on to my plate to verify my answer. After dinner came dishes and after dishes came Jeopardy and after Jeopardy came a chance for me to daydream. Many nights, around 8, my father would grab the crossword from the local paper and plop into the largest chair in the room. My mother would grab her ongoing knitting project and pick up where she left it the night before. I was given the boxy, wool loveseat in the corner of the room. The chair must have been passed down from my Great-Aunt Myrtle who probably stole the chair from a low-rate motel room in Buena Vista, Florida (I'm not saying Myrtle stole things; I'm just saying that the chair was old and gross). In this chair was where I spent the best portions of my days in that house.

For hours I would fight dragons, save good looking girls from quick moving trains, make game winning three-point shots. I was everything in that chair. In school I was nothing.

I guess *nothing* is a strong word, but I was certainly close. I had one true friend. I had too big a brain for the jocks and too small a brain for the geeks, so I settled for my imagination. I did play baseball, but it wasn't so much *playing* as it was *keeping score*. I was a four-year bench warmer. If it were up to me, I would come home from school everyday and sit in that smelly chair, but my dad would say, "You need to get some exercise. Go play a sport or something."

We settled on baseball. I was fairly good at it and I loved the fact that it had so much down time for the first 8 innings and then a grand finale in the 9th. For the first 8 innings I would sit and daydream or spit sunflower seeds. Then in the 9th I would stand and scream at the top of my lungs.

"C'mon pitch! Throw the deuce bay-bee!" or "Datta boy! Hit'em where dey ain't kid!" or "Ahn-ee Con-ee Pon-ee!" I liked that one. It made the players think I was cool. I wasn't. Every few games, coach would let me pinch hit if we were up by six runs or more. I had a career batting average of .600. I was 6 for 10. Let's see Barry Bonds hit .600 for a career. But, coach didn't care. I was nothing.

On that particular night, December 22nd, in my chair, I was thinking about what a curious sport auto racing is. I imagined what it would take to be a good racer and if I became one. I imagined myself coming home from school one day with my mother crying in the driveway. She would look at me and say, "We're sending you away Frankie. You're going to be a racecar driver whether you like it or not. It's a better life for you."

I turned to ask her is she thought it was neat that 'racecar' was spelled the same backward and forward, but she pressed a finger to my mouth and sobbed, "Go. Go before I change my mind."

So I went. I was sent on a plane to Italy because, according to my daydream, that's the only thing they do there. I got off the plane and a slick-haired European man revved up in a new Lamborghini. I giggled because he looked just like The Fonze, but I didn't tell him that because he probably had never watched Happy Days. He took off his expensive sunglasses and spit in a suave accent, "Rool noombair vun. Alvays press zie petal to zie metal," and then proceeded in doing such.

I think his accent was German, which really didn't make sense for the area of Europe we were in, but I didn't question his knowledge of driving. We were going an obscene amount of kilometers per hour when I looked at the speedometer, but since I didn't really know what that translated to in MPH, I just enjoyed the scenery. The man looked over at me and said, "Rool noombair doo. Alvays keep your hands at zen and doo." I looked at him and started laughing hysterically.

"Vas ist so funny?" he asked.

Out of a guffaw I tried to answer, "Because. Of all the things a professional racecar driver needs to know, the second most important is what my grandma tells me when I drive her to get her groceries."

"Okay dokay hot shot. Lets zie you try."

Well, it turned out I was a natural. I won the first twenty races I entered in and it was time to return to the American Circuit. I entered in the Indianapolis 500 and sent my mom and dad tickets to watch me. I was leading the race for 496 laps until a greasy guy from Seattle cut me off and spun me around. (I didn't know he was from Seattle. I just assumed because he was sponsored by Starbucks and reeked of fish). So there I was in the middle of the track, 4 laps to go, facing the wrong direction. I was about to give up. Just then, I looked out my window and saw my mom, she was yelling something. I took a closer look at her mouth and she said in slow motion, "Racecar." I knew exactly what to do.

I slammed the gear stick into reverse and drove the rest of the race backwards, just like "racecar". Needless to say, I won in dramatic fashion.

As I hoisted my jug of milk to the crowd, I came back to reality. My mom had turned off the radio and had gone to finish cleaning up the kitchen. "Another successful daydream accomplished," I thought as I went up to bed.

This was my routine. This is what made me tick. When I was younger my parents told me that it was unhealthy to just sit and make up things in your head. As I grew older, they found it was the only thing that calmed me down. I tried reading the paper, watching television, even knitting for God's sake, but nothing helped. The doctors of course told them it was ADD, so when my parents found out that I could stay calm by daydreaming instead of paying $500 for pills ever month, they never bugged me again. The other upside is that I always slept well. My friends would talk about dreams that woke them up or having cases of insomnia before exam days. I didn't know anything about those nights. Well, at least until December 22nd.

That night, I had my first dream. It startled me at first. I woke up with a look like a smelly sock was under my nose. I was confused. My body was hunched up and bracing against the mattress. I cross my legs Indian-style and cracked a smile. I had my first dream and it was good. My mind started rekindling the memory.

The school's halls were dark with a single lit lamp holding up its end of the bargain to give me enough visual access to move ahead. As I crept forward past the fire

engine red lockers, I saw her. She came out of the
Chemistry Lab and was headed towards the cafeteria to
my left. She gave me a quick, giddy look as she opened
the door and slipped inside. Her name was Angela
Pumpermyer. I followed into the noise of the cafeteria
and sat at my usual table. My lunch group, consisting of
Tom, wasn't there yet, probably getting extra help from a
teacher, so I decided to start my salami on rye without
him. Just as I started to indulge myself with the Italian
masterpiece, she was upon me. There, only 2 feet to my
left, was Angela standing, staring, looking directly at me.
My mouth wanted to droop down and join the rest of my
body but my brain reminded it of its function and it
continued to chew. Angela spoke.

"D'you mind if I sit here." She was slightly nervous.

"Ss-sure." I was especially nervous.

"I just thought you might like some company until
your friend get here."

"Thanks," I said honestly.

For the next few, odd minutes we talked about
anything. She was in a couple of my classes and we
seemed to have some things in common with movies. I
didn't remember most of our conversation because I was
secretly praying that Tom died in a freak Calculus
explosion. Then it happened. Somewhere between the
discussions of Chemistry and James Bond she froze me.

"Hey Frank, I was just wondering, um, if you, um,
wanted to go to the Prom with me?"

I woke up.

As I sat there in bed, I was ecstatic. My cheeks were touching my ears and my heart was driving faster than my slick-haired Italian friend. I had my first dream and it was beautiful. I had the worst sleep of my life that night, but I didn't care.

The next few weeks of winter break went by without consequence. My daily ritual was only interrupted by occasional visits from Tom or dentist appointments. School started and I became more nervous. As I drowsily hiked into school that first morning, I saw Angela standing next to her locker talking to friends. I grabbed a glance as I walked past, but I couldn't say anything. The truth was that she and I had the most intimate relationship I've ever experienced, and it was only a dream. I had to play it cool. That day in Chemistry class, Mr. Gerkin announced the new assignment.

"You will be working in teams of two to find the pH values of an assortment of household chemicals. Frankie. Pumpermyer. You're my Group 1."

My body jerked so fast that my left arm shot out and knocked a stack of beakers off the table. I apologized to the teacher and the teacher apologized to Angela.

For a week, I was going to be inches from her with only bleach and iodized salt keeping me focused. Fortunately, I managed to get by. We held light conversation and performed excellent titrations, I mean, mixed stuff well. She was gorgeous. Her thick, brunette hair was always gently resting on her shoulders and her upper teeth were always biting her bottom lip and teasing me from across the room. Every time she blinked, the world became slow motion to me.

On the Friday that we were finishing up our last mixture of the very poisonous Drain-O and the super-nucleic Apple Cider Vinegar, she gently removed her safety glasses and said, "Hey Tom, what are you doing this weekend."

Nothing of course.

"Nothing of course," I said.

That wasn't supposed to be out loud.

"Would you like to go to the movies with me and a couple friends? I just thought, since we have to talk a little about our report, we could do it while were waiting for the movie or something."

I was impressed at her skill of bullshitting. It's very hard to come by these days. "Sure, sounds great. What do you want to see?"

She looked at me and said, "Actually I think we were planning on seeing that new James Bond film."

Luckily, there were no beakers around me this time, but my eyes got very big and a voice inside my head was now mouthing "Holy crap" in slow motion. She must have been blinking.

This was getting too creepy. I didn't know what to do so I smiled and said, "Cool." That's what popular kids do, right? They say "cool".

On Saturday, we made it through the movie with minimal awkwardness and I returned home to sit in my chair. I didn't daydream though, I thought about my *real* dream. I wondered if I should invoke something, or stay calm and go with the flow, or transfer to another school because I was getting freaked out. The next day, it all got decided for me.

There I was, in Chemistry. At the end of class I went to my locker, Angela stayed behind to talk to the teacher. As I put my books away I slammed the door and turned to my left. For some reason half the lights had just gone out in the hallway. As I took one stride forward, she was there, coming from the Chemistry lab. It was happening all over again. She went to the cafeteria, I followed. Tom was not there, so she came and sat down instead. We talked about stuff, I didn't listen. But somewhere in between Chemistry and James Bond, she said it.

Now I know why my mouth dropped so hard. I didn't know whether to say yes or slap myself in the face. Out of good judgment I said "yes".

And that's when my life got a lot more interesting.

3

    I traveled back home after school that day through a remarkably warm January sun. I strolled at a slow, eight paces per minute because my mind was churning. I was mystified, but happy. While I walked home, I managed to convince myself that the day had all been a strange coincidence and returned to stories of dragons and brave heroes that night in my chair.

    Over the next few months Angela and I continued to date. I found very much pride in being able to call her my girlfriend and she found very much humor in calling me hers. I couldn't help but think every once in a while about how we came to be at this point and then I quickly would pass it off for fantasy or coincidence. It felt like a teenager who stops believing in Santa Clause but still misses the presents. Then summer came and I had too much else to think about.

In June, the trees were hot with leaves and bugs, and the wind had taken a backseat to children playing and cars honking. I still managed to take a few moments of my day to spend in my chair, but my time there was usually interrupted by a phone call or an unexpected knock from Angela. I didn't mind. For once in my life, I was living my stories instead of making them up. Everything was spontaneous for me; new and bold.

I remember July 4th that year very well. Angela and I had taken her new car to the county fair. It rained that night and mud sprayed all down her fresh paint. I thought it was very funny and she grinned it off and said, "I guess it had to get dirty sometime." We kissed under the fireworks when the rain slowed and I told her I loved her for the first time. She giggled and agreed. It was classic. Unfortunately, I remembered that night for other reasons.

On July 4th, I had my second dream.

After she dropped me off that night, I snuck up to my room and eased into my sheets. The pillows were just right, the moon gave me the perfect lighting, and I thought it would be the best sleep of my life. At 2:48 am I shot up and gasped for air.

My pillows were no longer cool, but were warm and heavy in my sweat. Beads of heat were falling down my bangs and in my mouth was my salt. I looked out the window at the moon which now looked dimmer than before. I took a hard swallow and tried to find my place in time and space. The dream was loud and clear. I broke the silence in the room and let it spill out.

"I'm going to hit the game winning homerun in the State Championship." I almost said it like a question.

It was so absurd, I wanted to laugh at the idea and go back to my sheets, but I looked down and realized I was shaking now. I crept downstairs and finished a glass of water. I looked in the mirror at a ghost. I was pale and thin. I hobbled back to my room and sat in the dark. My mind filed over the images of the dream. It was at Granger Field, the grass was cut just right and the infield was a little bit grainy, but not bad for the dry weather we had had. The game was at night, and as I sat there long enough, I could see the other team's faces; it was our district rivals, the Knights. I could see my coach look at me with his faded blue windbreaker that said Rockets across it. He sighed "You're in Frankie." It wasn't a happy sigh, he was conflicted. I could feel myself shuffle into the batter's box, I could feel the weight of the bat, and the noise of the crowd on my head. Then I felt the ball hit my bat.

I took in a deep breath and lied back down. It was time to sleep.

The next day was not so pleasant. Angela stopped by, cheerful as usual, and I tried to act the same. The entire day, I could never lift my smile high enough for her approval and she finally asked me what was wrong. I wanted to tell her my dreams, how we met, why I couldn't hold a smile. But I was too proud for that.

"I'm fine, just tired," I lied. She let it go.

At home I pressed my fingers to my forehead as if to force in common sense and realism, things I had spent my whole life chasing away. I forced myself to believe that my dreams were, just that, dreams. Meeting Angela was coincidence. The baseball game was impossible. Maybe the time I had been spending away from my chair was now entering into my subconscious. Again, I chose maturity over innocence, and the days moved much faster.

It was now spring. My senior year of high school was becoming an hour glass of my life. Angela and I were better than ever, my classes were finishing up, and four colleges had already accepted me. The hour glass had one more grain of sand to drop.

I don't remember what happened during the day on April 3rd, but I remember the night. I remember getting on my last bus ride as a baseball player heading towards the State Championship. Again this season, I was designated to keep the bench warm, getting a total of 5 and 1/3 innings of playing time, but I didn't mind. I enjoyed the smell of dirt, wet socks, and chewing tobacco. I enjoyed wearing a jersey to school on Fridays. I enjoyed the first 8 peaceful innings of every game. Tonight was no different. It was the top of the 9ᵗʰ now and our team was in the field. We were down by a half dozen runs and we were all out of pitchers. Coach sent in our southpaw to try and close out the inning. Two strikeouts later, the opposing team's bruiser step up to the plate. Their bruiser went by the name of Pop, and could do just that if he got a hold of a curveball.

Our southpaw threw a curveball.

Pop injected a slice of hell through the baseball and sent it on a rope towards our second baseman, Willy. Willy caught the ball in the bare leather of the glove and hit the ground. The fans started cheering at such an unbelievable grab, but fell silent when Willy screamed in agony. He yelled curses and held his hand. The rest of the team trotted back to the dugout and eventually Willy followed; his palm blue and black. Coach looked down the roster and sighed, "You're in Frankie".

I thought I heard him say it, but didn't move because I thought I was hallucinating.

"God Dammit Frank! Get your helmet on and get in the box!"

This was much clearer. I approached coach gently and wondered out loud, "Why me coach?"

"Because we have no one left that's allowed to reenter for Willy, and he's up next. So that means you're up! Got it?"

"Yessir." I fumbled for an extra helmet and fumbled some more for a bat and fumbled some more trying to remember how to hit a baseball. My mind was blank. I got into the batter's box against a lean, smooth right-hander who threw strike-one before I realized where I was. I felt like an asthma patient running through a saw dust factory. I swung at the next pitch, but late. I looked over to the coach for signs. He wasn't looking at me. Strike-three came in the form of a fastball on the outside corner. I did not swing, but I enjoyed watching such a beautiful pitch from this angle. I slightly wished I had my camera as I shuffled back to the dugout to murmured "Nice Tries" or "Get'm Next Times". There wasn't going to be a next time and I was content with that.

The entire night I had been holding onto the dream in the back caves of my mind. Finally, I could confront it. "It was just a dream," I smiled. I felt like a great weight was lifted from my shoulders. My teammates around me were solemn. Like a funeral. I was comfortable. Like a bowl of warm soup.

Ping! Our catcher hit a double into left field.

My teammates were drained and tired. I felt like doing a jig.

Ping! Our shortstop answered with a single into right.

My teammates were watercolor on a plastic canvas. I was paint-by-number.

Ping! A pop up to the pitcher, dropped!

My teammates were smiling. I was...what? Smiling?

Ping! Another double through the gap. Ping! Another. Ping! Another.

I was just taking off my helmet when I heard it like a WWII tank. Another Ping! and then a roar from our crowd. A homerun from our left fielder brought us within two runs. The next batter then hammered a line drive over the first baseman's head and the cheering continued.

As our designated hitter strolled to the plate, someone yelled, "Hey Frankie, get a helmet on. You're up next, kid." My mouth was a cod fish. I did as I was told and grabbed a bat and helmet and found my way to the warm-up circle. As I watched in horror for the next few moments I felt a calm come over me, although it didn't help, but I felt as if something were saying to me, "it's going to be okay."

The opposing pitcher kicked a long stride and hurled a fireball into the ribs of our hitter. And so it was.

The cheers were deafening, yet I still heard my cleats comb the sand as I strutted into the box.

The outfield lights were scorching far in the distance, yet I was blind to everything in front of me.

I watched longingly as the opposing coach changed out pitchers and replaced the lean boy with the bruiser, Pop. As he warmed up, my bones gasped for more air each time his pitch hit the catcher's mitt. With each thud, my body flinched like a cruel game of Russian roulette. My coach held onto his stern look, but nothing more, no encouragement. I felt naked. Again I stepped into the box. I gripped the bat like my uncle taught me in 3rd grade.

"Line up your knuckles. There you go. Now when you swing, throw your wrists first and then let your hips follow."

The first pitch was low and away. I liked to think I let it go on purpose, but the truth was I wasn't ready yet. I stepped out of the box once more to take a final deep breath and back in I went, back to the trenches, back to the graveyard shift.

The bruiser's mouth let go of a large amount of tobacco, and his arm let go of the ball. I picked it up right away, the seams, end over end; a fastball. I threw my wrists and let my hips follow. I felt the beautiful connection of metal on rawhide and for that very instant, I was glad I was not holding my camera.

I hit the shit out of the ball.

The announcer's exact words were, "Oh my god, he hit a homerun. I'm not sure who *he* is, but he hit a homerun." As I dropped my bat and headed to first base, he was still scrounging for his stat sheet. "Uh, it says here, uh, yes. His name is Frank, and he has just hit the game winning homerun in the State Championship."

4

I know all of this probably does not impress you or send shivers through your body like it did me, but everything has a beginning, and you need to know mine. Like these raisins, I started with something great; I had witnessed two miracles in my life before I had turned 18. I was a grape that summer before I went to college. My chest was always stuck out when I walked. My thoughts of weakness were turned into thoughts of power and discipline.

I became too grownup for my chair. The chair saw the signs, it knew I couldn't stay there forever, but it was still sad. The day I left for school, the chair was more mute and dull than ever, I can't say that I felt the same. I was off to bigger places, better things.

I often think back about that chair and the hours I spent wasting life in it. It reminds me of the chair I am in right now, at this party. It seems to be personable, looks like it has been shared by a few generations. I'm sure it has seen drama and persona that others have not; romantic evenings, family quarrels, the growing older of a child.

It is odd to me to believe that life can not be as simple as sitting and watching. You must participate to actually find life. I looked in the dictionary the other day to see what it had to say.

"Ah hem," the dictionary cleared its throat, "Life is the condition that distinguishes organisms from inorganic objects and dead organisms."

"Is that it?" I beckoned, "Life is just simply how to tell if you are not dead?"

"Precisely," retorted my dictionary.

"So in that case, you are not alive..."

"Well..."

"The pages in your body, they don't breathe..."

"Now, hold on th-"

"Your spine, it doesn't bend and think like mine can."

"True, bu-"

24

"You are nothing but an inorganic pile of ink and tree!" I shouted.

With that, the book was silent.

A fair girl took a seat and a beer next to me a few minutes ago, I asked her name and what she thought the definition of life was. She is talking to another guy now, and the raisins still look delicious.

I'm not saying I know the answer to everything; in fact that's why I am writing this novel, to help me understand it more myself. I want to understand why things happen, not just where, at what time, and to whom. I want to be able to see my life as a drawing board that is half painted, and me, standing over it, holding a brush.

My last summer at home was spent with Angela and my car. I headed out the door in August on my way to a technology school in Washington D.C. I had not quite seen life yet. My painting was just getting started.

My morning train stopped at Foggy Bottom Station and I flung my body into the stiff breeze. I knelt down outside the platform to tie my left shoe. There was a golden red leaf lying next to the hand rail. "Probably the last of year," I thought to myself. I picked it up and it was frozen to the touch and broke in my hand into a thousand crackled pieces that fell to the cement like snow.

Two and a half years I had been in college. Two and a half years I had been working a part time job to pay for it. Two and a half years of riding the train, day in, day out, clickity clack, clickity clack. Today was a Tuesday. I was working today.

I showed up to the office early so I could get a newspaper and flip through a time warp of images with war and politics and designer fashion. I worked at a mediocre engineering firm, Brown and Sherman Attorneys. I spent half of my time there correcting blueprints and the other half making my own. It wasn't a great gig, but it paid well and looked good on a resume.

At five o'clock, back to the train. Clickity clack, clickity clack. My apartment was calm and dead, just as I had left it. I put a pot on the stove and started a festive dinner of noodles and bread. It was an important night, an anniversary. Exactly 8 months, 21 days, and 23 hours ago, Angela left my life. Now I just had noodles.

I sat on the couch at nine and poured some bourbon. It smelled like calm and dead, just as I had left it. I crawled into my bed at ten but didn't close my eyes until eleven. I didn't daydream anymore, I just sat, and stared, and sat, and gritted my teeth, and sat, and cried. I no longer had any spark in my life. I was distant from the world around me that had kites, and dogs, and flashing neon lights that said, "Dry Cleaners". The bourbon swam down my stomach and exploded into a fiery mass of napalm that clung to my throat. My mind was blurred and clinging from motion. At this, I fell unconscious into a sad focus of sleep.

I awoke at seven and put the night behind me. The station was crowded with strangers today bundled up in layers of fabric that did not match in any way, but they were warm. I wore a gray pea coat and black slacks that neither shielded me from the wind nor made me seem tasteful. I was calm and dead.

Onto the train I stepped behind a larger, bald man and a pair of young girls listening to rap. Clickity clack, clickity clack. The rap was dimmed by their headphones so all I heard were the tempo of the hi-hat and the acoustics of the rapper's lyrics. They nodded their head to a beat that was not my own and the bald man stared at the floor. As the train approached Metro Center Station, I saw a leaf under my seat. It was also golden red but much warmer than the leaf I encountered the day before.

I got off the train and moved down the escalator towards the eastbound platform. The woman on the intercom announced, "We are experiencing delays in our Eastbound-Westbound services. We apologize for the inconvenience. Again, we are experiencing delays in our Eastbound-Westbound services." A dozen sighs could be heard in any given area of the terminal. I did not mind, so I sat and stared.

The train arrived and the groans and the rustling of overcoats sifted into the doorways. I entered into the first car and settled right behind the driver because I liked looking out the front as we rode. I was nearly the last one on the train. *Nearly.* There was a young, yet wrinkled man that stepped on after me with his hands buried in his pockets. He had a torn, mauve leather jacket and a three-day old beard. Just above his deep set eyes was the edge of a black wool cap. He nudged though me aggressively to stand at the closer end of the window. He spoke.

"Shut down the train and don't even speak," he directed the driver. The driver was a larger, less gentle, black woman who had not yet had her morning coffee. Their eyes met and his followed hers down towards his right hand in which he was holding a small handgun.

I saw it now too. The driver's face choked back and whispered, "Oh my God."

The man spoke. "Shut down this train and I won't hurt anybody." He was calm and dead. I watched as the driver turned a key and felt the train let out a breath of air. At this, the crowd perked towards the front of the car. They too saw the gun. Many women sobbed and many men fell into seats. The man spoke.

"Alright everybody. I would like you to take out your wallets and watches and jewelry and pass them up here to me very slowly. If you cooperate, this won't take long, and you can be on your way without any harm." The man took one step in front of me and held his gun in plain sight.

I reacted.

I grabbed the man's fist holding his gun and simultaneously drilled my right knee into his back. My finger's crawled up to the trigger and pulled once to make sure the gun was loaded. A blast and a scar ripped through the roof of the train and more women screamed. I could feel the man flinch at the power of his own weapon and I locked his ankles, sending him to the ground. When his head hit, he lost enough grip on the gun to allow me to swipe the cold instrument and slide it ahead on the floorboard. Another passenger quickly picked it up and clicked on the safety clasp.

The man started struggling and tried to throw an elbow towards me. I pushed it past my body and connected a heavy fist into his jaw. The man did not speak.

I stood up and many women were smiling and many men were cheering. My eyes followed the men and women down the length of the car, and as I did a smile tainted my face. I could feel again, the warm, the excitement. More applause rose and for a second I was almost happy. *A second.*

My smile disappeared at the end of the car. Through the glass two men in similar tattered gear were staring at me and shuffling out of the second car.

"Get down! Everybody stay down!" I instructed. Many passengers turned and saw the two men. Both had equally ravenous handguns drawn upon the train. I knew what I had to do.

"Toss me the gun," I ordered the passenger still clutching the device. It landed in my palms and I rotated it in my hands like a baseball. I unlocked the safety and held it tightly with both hands in front of my body like a lit candle. I leaned through the doorway and took aim at the floor in front of the men's feet. I fired. Two shots rang out through the terminal and the men scattered back into the second car. I tossed the gun back to the passenger and said "Shoot them if they chase me." I took off in a sprint.

There were almost thirty meters to the nearest staircase and I slid into it just as a shot grazed the cement wall next to me. My plan was to get the two men to follow me just enough to have my friendly passenger shoot them down when they moved out of the car. As I peered behind my wall to the staircase, I watched as the closest man was snipped from behind and fell to the cement grabbing his back. My passenger missed high on the second man. To my right a large police officer was also in pursuit and fired another quick shot at the man. I pivoted on my left foot and took off running when his bullet missed the target. The race began.

I lead in front, with coattails flying, the gunman close behind, and a misfit policeman trying to keep up with the chase. I barreled up the stairs and heard another shot ring off the hand rail as I slipped around another corner. A 100 meter dash ensued as I sprinted down the westbound platform. As I ran, I shouted words towards others, "Get out of here! He has a gun! Get away! Get away!" Some listened and moved. Some were doubters and didn't leave the scene until they saw the man and the gun, flying wildly. I looked back and saw vengeance and sweat on his face. As I bobbed in and out of the cement pillars holding up the room, I heard no shots or screaming. The man was after me only. I felt sick.

I turned another corner and he fired another shot. This one snatched part of my waist and I rolled, shoulder first, into the cement. I hobbled up and continued running. My vision was slowly getting blacker with pain. The intercom came on again.

"Your next northbound train to Shady Grove. Your next northbound train to Shady Grove."

In front of me was a ledge that dropped down thirty feet onto the northbound tracks. To the right and left of me were walls. Solid walls. Behind me, I heard foot patter lean into my direction. One shot missed my head. I was still running. I took a much longer stride and sprung over the ledge towards the top of the northbound train. At first glance I saw no train and only tracks waiting for my arrival. Then the train was under me, catching my body, and pushing me off onto the stiff ground. The brakes screamed and I landed on the platform in a heap of abnormal mass. I shifted my head just enough to watch my pursuer take aim and then get struck in the back by the police officer. He was calm and dead.

The northbound train unloaded and people crowded my view of the ceiling. My breath was heavy and blood was spilling out of my side and shoulder. I closed my eyes to a whirlwind of faded color and loudness. I fainted.

I woke up ten minutes later with paramedics over my body. A cloth had already bandaged my waist and a young girl was speaking.

31

"He's up. He's up. Okay sir, you're going to be alright. We're going to put you on this stretcher."

I let out a grunt that sounded like I was eating a doughnut. She smiled at this and reminded me again that I would be fine. I caught a glimce of her legs as she went to get more tape and I agreed that I might ask her to date me if I was in a better condition. At this I smiled and tumbled back into sleep.

The trip onto the stretcher, up the stairs, into the ambulance, and into a hospital bed was too jumbled for me to recall, but I arrived safe. The drugs wore off around 2 pm. A doctor was there. *He* did not have nice legs. My first words were, "Do you know the number of that paramedic at the station."

He smiled and said, "Well Frank, you've had quite a morning."

5

The writers from the Daily Tribune were the first to interrupt my room after the police were done with their questioning. Flashes lit up my face and small men with porkpie hats smelled like pastrami. I tried to calm them the best I could so I could retell the story at my own speed. They tried to throw in their own pieces of gold.

"Frank, is it true that the first killer had a KKK patch on his jacket?"

"Frank, did you say that the police officer at the station was too 'pudgy' to catch up to the pursuer?"

"Frank, did you have this escape tactic of yours planned out ahead of time just in case?"

To be honest, it was hard to recall anything that happened more than I had explained before. The morning was so short, so detail-less. Ten minutes into the interview, I paused when a reporter asked me what the criminals looked like. I couldn't remember. I remembered the leather jacket, the hat, and the guns; but no faces, no out-of-the-ordinary features to speak of. I felt alone, as if all of it didn't really happen, as if this was just another dream. But it wasn't a dream.

The next day, the newspaper proved that. There I was, on the front page with a half-smiling picture that read "College Student Disarms Thief; Outthinks Two More". I read the first couple of paragraphs until the writer went on a tangent discussing gun laws in America. I folded the paper away.

I remained in the hospital room until noon that day. My parents called around 10 am when they finally got news of what had happened. They were furious. My mom was furious at the audacity of some 'thugs', as she called them, trying hurt her little boy. My dad needed to know when I would be coming home and leaving that 'pitiful' city. I assured them I would not be leaving and I was very capable and conscience of my own well-being. They did not call again that day.

After a large meal courtesy of the D.C. Police Department, I returned to my apartment and reapplied my bandages. Today was Wednesday, tomorrow I had work.

I got on the train Thursday morning to a swarm of stares and whispers. I knew it might take a while until everything was normal again. Clickity clack, clickity clack. My office was quiet and my co-workers stopped by to offer me some congratulatory blueprints to run through. I didn't mind, it kept me busy.

That night, I checked my bandages again. The place where the bullet went through was healing faster than I expected. The wound that entered my flesh reminded me of a jigsaw piece. The piece then wrapped around my side leaving a comet-like streak. It stung hard as I poured some more hydrogen peroxide over it. The evil liquid ran slowly over the red-black wound, teasing me, and then cascaded into the sink.

That night I crawled into an immobile, uncomfortable position in my bed so I could let my wound heal. I sat upright against three stacked pillows. They were old and brown and it made me think of my chair. The warm suffering made my mind trip over stories, not imaginary ones, but of my own story, happening right now. I tried to recall what exactly happened that morning on the train. I tried to remember the men's faces, my reaction to running out of the car, to holding a gun. Even more importantly, where were my dreams? This was a major part of my life and I reacted purely on instinct. There was no dream, not one I could remember anyway.

"Maybe I had the dream and just forgot it," I mumbled aloud. I had read a few weeks earlier that 90 percent of all dreams are had unnoticed. "Maybe, that's what happened. But it couldn't be! It hasn't ever happened before." I had so many questions and no where to look for answers. My mind tumbled and then stuck on another topic, something I'd been thinking over since the incident, when I was holding the gun.

I had never held a handgun before. I shot my grandfather's rifle out on his farm once when I was much younger, probably 11 or 12 years old.

"Okay Frank, this is the scope here," my grandfather said in a brute fashion. "Now you're gonna close your right eye and aim down the scope with your left. Take the butt of the gun and put it into your right armpit like this." He motioned and I thought he looked like a modern day John Wayne. My grandfather was tall and thick. I would imagine him to be a boxer in his younger days, but I never got that story, just the stories about the war and the factory; only cold stories. I jammed the rifle into my armpit.

"There ya go. Now your right hand next to the trigger, and your left eye down the scope."

My view traveled down the long barrel and onto my target - a red, hand-painted circle on an old piece of hickory board, propped up against a tree. My index finger gently felt its way onto the trigger and then, in an angry clench, blasted a bullet out of the gun. I hit the middle of the red.

"Whoa boy!" shouted my grandfather. "You're a natural, kid. Here, take some more."

He mimed the process of reloading a rifle and handed it back to me. I repeated the process of aiming and firing again. Boom! Another perfect shot. My grandfather laugh so hard he almost dropped the box of bullets he was holding.

"Here boy, we need to get you some more distance between that board." I followed him back to, what he called, fifty feet.

Aim. Trigger. Red again.

Again he moved me to eighty feet away.

Aim. Trigger. Red.

Before my first shot missed the red circle, I was more than two hundred feet away and missed only inches to the left. My grandfather was rolling. "Must have been the wind that time huh?" I smiled because he was smiling, and he only smiled when my grandmother cooked blackberry pie. I didn't know what it meant to hit the targets like I did, it seemed rather simple. I just looked and shot.

My grandfather died two months later. It was his heart. That day out at the farm, shooting at a red painted circle, was the last time I saw him really happy. When he died, he left me his rifle. My grandmother hated the thing and insisted I couldn't have it until I was older.

Thinking again about the morning on the train, I found a lot of comparisons to the shooting that rifle. I did something I never knew I could do, and did it perfectly. I made something out of nothing, like a raisin. My grandfather would have been proud.

I was smiling as I sat in bed for hours thinking, until I was finally struck down by exhaustion. My eye lids fell limp, my body molded down the pillows into a lazy incline, and my mouth went numb. At around 4 a.m., my eyes opened again and my body went vertical.

I had another dream. It was my third dream. Instead of waking up to shaking and sweat and white like my other dreams, I sat up calm and quiet. The dream was complicated, but I replayed it in my head as simply as shooting a rifle.

There was no noise in this dream, only actions. The dream started with me just standing and panting. I was in a room full of wires and metal. I looked around the corner and saw no one. My feet dashed across the room to an illuminated control panel and a million blinking switches. I started flipping a bright red switch until I heard a sound. I turned around and saw a very official looking man talking to me. Everything he said was muted. He walked closer to me, still talking, and looked into my eyes sternly. I felt the ground shake hard beneath me and the dream became audible. The man was completely calm. His eyes were bright and anxious.

"Go ahead Frank. You're about to save the world."

I woke up.

6

We were inside the Chinese restaurant now. It was called Lucky Buddha. Tom was curious.

"Who's the novel going to be about?"

I didn't want to tell him it was going to be about me. He would think I was going crazy, or close to it. So I made something up.

"It's about a kid who has dreams that come true in real life," I said confidently.

The Tambourine had to jingle her two cents into the discussion. "My uncle wrote a novel once and it was about a woman who could turn into a lioness on command. She was born in the jungle but learned to speak English and took over Parliament."

I was amazed at how annoying the Tambourine could be.

Fortunately, Tom also disapproved of her absurd fact-of-the-day and reversed the conversation back to my book. "So when are you going to start writing this novel?"
"Tonight."

There was a picture of the president on the wall behind Tom with an autograph. I looked around and there were more leaders and icons, all with their arms around the owner of this dim-lit, mediocre Chinese diner we were currently slurping noodles at. Then I caught a glimpse of a picture with Elvis and I concluded the pictures were fake. The menu read 'Est. 1993'. I put down my smile and looked across the table to Tom.

"Tom, I'm going away tomorrow. I joined the Army a few months ago and they have a group leaving tomorrow for Basic Training in Charleston, South Carolina."

Tom's reaction was not of surprise, like I thought it would be, but of concern. He opened his mouth to speak and then pursed his lips and let out air from his nose. He never looked up from his teriyaki.

"I know it's kind of sudden, but I've been in kind of a rut lately, and I just *need* this right now. I can't really explain more than that."

Tom nodded in understanding. "I know Frank, but the Army? Have you really thought about this?"

"Of course I've thought about this." I hadn't really. "And plus, the Army isn't much involved anymore. I read yesterday that we're bringing home more and more troops everyday. And the ones that are still fighting are mostly pilots; hardly anyone's fighting in hand-to-hand combat anymore."

Gina chimed in. "Yeah, my cousin is in the Air Force and he says that all they have to do to now is to fly over a target and push two buttons; one to activate the missiles, and one to fire them. The rest is done through the computers in the plane."

"See." I hated taking sides with Gina, but I was unsure and needed a second opinion.

Tom went back to pursing his lips. He looked like my father sitting there. He scratched his whiskers with his knuckles. His hands were always balled up in his sleeve and he always looked cold. He thought a moment and then gave his verdict. His voice sounded like a last resort. "What if you are flying a plane over the desert and you come onto a small village? Your commanding officer is in your ear and tells you there might be a militia group staked out there. You recognize the village and know that there is nothing there that is more harmful than a stray dog. Do you push the button Frank?"

I bit my lip. "N-no, of course not." I stuttered.

"But it's an order; you could get dismissed from the military and even put in jail or worse."

"N-no, I wouldn't do it. I-I would say the m-missile malfunctioned or something." I was lying and Tom could pick up my bluff.

He sat back and grinned, "Okay bud. I believe you. Just don't get yourself killed out there okay."

"Sure thing".

Tom's remarks reminded me of a party I went to when I was very young. Not a "cool" party with college kids and raisins, but one that my father took me to. He took me in his car one night without telling me where we were going. He had a lot of mysteries like that. We pulled up to a small brick house with a broken shutter next to the door. I knocked first and a grizzly man peeked his beard through the crevice of the door.

"Hey Danny," the Grizzly said.

"Hey Roy," my father said.

We were ushered into the hall and around the corner. There were no people in any other part of the house, but when we went around the corner it looked like an Aerosmith concert. The room at the end of the hall was busting, not with noise, but with adults, just standing.

"Sorry about bringing Frank," my father started. "His mother was at a PTA meeting tonight."

"It's alright," said the Grizzly. "You know the drill."

I did not like the drill.

"Okay son, you need to stay out here in the hall and sit. You can listen all you want to the adults, but don't look. Okay?" I nodded and found a good piece of wall to crouch against. I sat and stared and listened.

"Sorry I'm late guys. Where's Benny? There you are. Come here bud." I could hear the man called Benny squeak across the hardwood floors and then heard the patting of a manly hug. The people must have been waiting on my father because no one had talked since he

42

entered the room and now he was the only one who would.

"Thank you, ladies and gentlemen for coming on such short notice. As all of you unfortunately heard today, Benny is leaving for the war tomorrow. He's been called up for a stint in Baghdad and, well, he's leaving first thing in the morning."

I heard sniffles and heavy breathing like women crying. I faced the doorway to see who was crying, but the Grizzly boxed up the entire frame. I continued to listen.

Another man got up and said a prayer. Then, the people seemed to start moving around because the wood was creaking loudly now. Still the only voices heard were those of people addressing Benny.

One woman sobbed, "Good luck over there Benny. Don't get yourself killed, okay?"

"I won't." That was the first time I heard Benny's voice. It was much younger and softer than I had expected it to be. More and more adults offered Benny his or her own simple piece of knowledge to take with him on his trip. But, most were the same. There was a general trend of not dieing and good lucks. Occasionally, someone would throw in a "God bless you" or a "fight for freedom." The wallpaper and I became best friends for that night. It even seemed sad. The splotches on the ceiling were getting larger every second staining the already boring piece of tan decoration. I sat there for a short time before my father slid out of the crowd and past the Grizzly. The Grizzly shook my father's hand tightly without saying a word and then turned to me.

"See ya around Frankie." I didn't know anything. The Grizzly, Benny, the house. But everyone seemed to know my father, and therefore, me. I felt honored and shunned at the same time. I learned nothing that night except that my father was an important man and that war made people sad. I think that is all my father wanted me to learn.

A week later a postcard came to the house from Benny. When my parents weren't looking and I swiped the card and read it under the kitchen table. The card was simple and quick.

> *I am still in Norfolk, but have finished nearly all the processing. Tomorrow we'll get our uniforms and PT gear and do our final check out. Saturday morning we'll leave at 0730 for Ft. Jackson by bus. I had four vaccinations on Tuesday, smallpox, anthrax, Tetanus-diphtheria and Hepatitis B so I felt like a human pincushion but I'm good to go.*
> *Take Care,*
> *Benny Angel*

I never had actually seen Benny Angel. But his words and his life captivated me. At my young age, to actually *know* a soldier, I was proud. One night at dinner, I asked about Benny. My father lowered the fork from his mouth and looked across the table to my mother. Both couldn't find any words.

Finally my father said, "He's doing fine, Bud. Why?"

I told him that it would be fun to be a soldier. My mother slammed the table and yelled, "Just eat your peas, Frank."

"B-but..."

My father stared at me and sternly said, "Frank the Army is not a life you want, someday you'll understand this. So until then, I don't want you mentioning Benny or any war in this house. Okay?"

"Yes sir." From then on, I would be more secretive about reading Benny's letters. They came every two weeks or so. I would check the mail everyday when I got home until the postcard came. The second postcard was lying on top of the counter one day after school. There was a palm tree on the front.

I'm here at beautiful Ft. Jackson, SC having completed my first full day of the Navy Combat Training Course which in reality is Army training. We have a 48 pound vest of body armor we wear on top of our DCUs then we put a load bearing vest on top of that. We have the Kevlar helmet with goggles. Plus all the other gear, sleeping bag, mattress, boots, canteens, etc. its four duffle bags of gear. We got gear issue today, did some PT and got weapons. I have a 9mm to keep plus an M16

*to train with but I'll return it before I leave
here.*

     Take care,
      Benny

After that postcard, there wasn't another one for a month. I got worried that maybe my parents had started hiding the cards from me. I searched all over to no success. Finally, on a Tuesday, a card came.

     *Sorry about no updates lately but it's
been busy and for some reason the OWA
wasn't working. We finished our weapons
training last week. I qualified on the 9mm
pistol as a sharpshooter which is my
mandatory weapon. You're right; I have to give
the M16 back on Thursday. I tried to qualify
anyway, but fell short by 4 hits. I may get a
chance to try again.*

     *Yeah, the gear is heavy and hot and
you sweat and sweat so you constantly drink
water and fluids all day long because if you
don't you'll be in serious trouble. We have a
water bladder we carry on our backs called a
camelback with a tube over our shoulder so
we can drink anytime we need to.*

     *This is my last week here. Monday we
get to shoot heavy weapons, the 50 cal
machine gun, the 240 and 249 automatic*

*weapons and the 40 mm grenade launcher.
Fun! Then we'll do convoy training, land
navigation, urban warfare and some
classroom work before finishing on Friday. I
could be leaving Friday night or Saturday or
later for Kuwait. I will find out my travel
itinerary on Wednesday.*

Take care,

Benny

Again there was a long wait between this card and
the next. One night at dinner, I let it slip. "Is Benny in
Kuwait yet?" My parents looked up from their dinner
again and argued with each other as if I wasn't in the
room.

"This is your fault," my mother started, "making it
so secretive. He's just being a curious boy."

"I know, I just wanted to protect him a little better.
I guess he does deserve to see it though. He's getting
older."

"And smarter. I think this once will be alright."

My father walked out of the room and came back
with another card. "Here you go, kid."

*My time here at Ft. Jackson is winding
down. I have completed the Navy Combat
Training under the watchful eye of numerous
Army drill sergeants. This week we did urban
combat, convoy protection, chemical warfare,
ate MREs, fired .50 caliber machine guns,*

marched several miles in full battle rattle, and ran PT. Boy am I tired!

Sunday, I fly to Kuwait and will arrive there Monday afternoon Kuwait time. I'll spend about 4 days there getting more training before finally heading to Balad Air Base Iraq for my duty assignment.

I hope everyone is doing well. I will let you know of my e-mail as soon as I get it.

Benny

That was the last card I ever read from Benny Angel. A few weeks later, I asked about him again at dinner. My mother started crying a little, but got up and left the table before me or my father could see her weakness. My father just shook his head at me as if to say, "Just drop it, son." I never asked about Benny Angel again.

The Tambourine missed the whole conversation due to a phone call and was sitting down just as Tom saluted me, half jokingly.

"Okay, so apparently there's a big party going on over at The Creek Apartments tonight. Everyone want to go, right?"

I looked at Tom and Gina and said, "Sure, why not?"

7

All around me are plain walls, plain bed sheets, plain soldiers. I am one of those plain soldiers. As I sit down to continue my story, my head is shaved, my eyes are heavy, and the flashlight in my bunk is struggling to give me enough light to finish. This is the only time I can write now, at 0200, when the world, and more importantly, the other soldiers, are asleep.

The only thing I brought with me from home was the beginning of my story. After a year and a half, I finally have time to write again. *Where am I?* I am in a bunker in the middle of East Germany. The year is 1946. Don't blink. Now I am in a helicopter floating

over Saigon. The year is 1975. Don't speak.
Now I am in the cavity of U.S. Naval Ship and
above is dying and loud and beauty. The
year is 1914 and I'm off the coast of Pearl
Harbor.

It doesn't matter where I am; I'm a
soldier in war. I am deaf to the feeling of
wind and sun. I am a killer. I remember
when I wasn't a killer, when I was a saint. I
was 21 and I just had a dream about saving
the world.

The next morning, my dream was still lingering on the
tips of my conscience. I ventured over to my stack of
post-it notes and stuck a new one to the refrigerator.

<u>To do:</u>
√ Take out trash
√ Do laundry
√ Study for physics test
Save the world

"Perfect." I smiled as I looked at my tasks at hand.
I had come to an understanding with my dreams. They
do what they want, I do what I want, and if we happen to
come together, the better off we are. If my dream of
saving the world didn't come true, I wouldn't be hurt, just
realistic. That's how I was now, numb.

I went back to fixing my bandages and eating a dull
breakfast. The eggs were too runny and the toast was too

not-toasty. I got on the train again that morning to a sea of people like me. Numb. They had long forgotten who I was. Yesterday's news. On the train, the coats were all dark and the faces were all weary beige. The only noise this morning was a wave of disapproving grunts that rolled down the length of the train when the operator announced "technical difficulties".

I always thought this was very amusing. No matter the racial, political, or spiritual background of a person, *everyone* hated public transportation. This was a fact. Once I saw a homeless man turn to an uptown attorney when the operator finished and said, "Damn, ain't nothing like public transportation to start your day with a smile." The attorney shot back with his own sarcasm.

"Yeah, they spend millions every year to plant trees in concrete, but they can't afford to give the subway a set of wheels, a new engine, and a decent driver." The homeless man nodded and laughed in approval and the two carried on complaining like college chums. The train again picked up speed and after a moment, the homeless man asked the attorney for a couple dollars.

The attorney put away his grin and scoffed at the beggar. He looked down at his Rolex and continued out the door towards another day of speed and money and spreadsheets. The homeless man nodded as he saw another friend leave his life. He was numb.

My time spent at work was mindless. There was no substance of creativity or expression. Even the most elaborate of blue prints seemed lifeless on the cold mornings. The lunch hours would go by without a single descent piece of food, and yet I was full. I would rush up the escalators coming off the subway and get home wondering what I was rushing for. There was nothing worth hurrying for in my life, nothing worth an extra ten minutes of my day. I again became a friend within myself. I returned to daydreaming.

I remember one night in particular. I was an astronaut and this was my life. I could see myself at an early age, learning about rockets. At 7, I built and launched my first successful rocket, a D-87. It was beautiful. A burst of yellow and white light shooting in the air followed by a mist of smoke. My parents were there. They could see the rocket farther than I could.

"Is it still going?" I yelled.

My father looked into the clouds, "Yeah son, it's way up there now."

When I grew older, the rockets got bigger as I got bigger. I launched patterns of simultaneous rockets at the state fair. They had blue and red smoke that could wrap like a Native American bracelet at 1000 feet. The crowds wanted more and so I worked hard giving them a show. At 17, people from Arkansas and Missouri were making the trip to our field. They wanted something in their life and they didn't know what. All they knew is that they liked the way my rockets skipped across the baby blue backdrop, creating timid works of art that drifted from town to town. Each launch was more and more a time for me to stop and be a kid again. My mouth always made an "O" shape as the rocket disappeared into infinity. I was like a little leaguer on Fourth of July all over again.

When I went to college, my major was certain. Aerospace Engineering. Not long after I began learning about propulsion of jet engines did a dark-skinned man from Dubai give me a job at NASA. I started with numbers. Plotting the trajectory of space travel on paper was like color by number on a black sheet. I could explore.

The more I explored, the more I found that needed exploring. When I turned 25, I became the youngest man in space, on my birthday no less. The mission control director was in my ear.

"T minus ten seconds."

My hands held tight to the resting bars.

"Nine."

I took a deep breath and let my bottom lip go limp.

"Eight...seven...six..."

The engines kicked and the view in front of me turned into a jumble of lights and sounds. The seat and the shuttle itself cringed at such power. My left brain wanted to calculate the thrust needed to ram us deep into the atmosphere. My right brain told the left brain to shut up and hang on.

"Five...four...three..."

Two more thrusters kicked. Outside, pillars were releasing off the side of the craft and millions of tons of steel pieces fell to the earth like paper off a piñata. The fire underneath was red hot with fury and the 18 layers of flame-deterrent foam made sure to calm the ensuing explosion from reaching the ship.

"Two..."

Boom! The final set of pillars broke off and shrunk to the turf. I gripped tighter and started laughing to myself. Images of my first rollercoaster and first spring off a diving board and my first kiss were all being rolled into a giant ball of anxiety.

"One. Liftoff."

Earth. Space. That is what it felt like. The vibrations running through my spine made it less of a joyride and more of an experiment never to be tried again. I threw up in my helmet.

In space, I could see the earth and I found my house with a pencil tip and a hard squinting exercise. I laughed with my colleagues when jello floated around the cabin and I laughed some more when we hid behind the moon, like playing a game of tag with the planets. This was a moment I could never forget. And so I came out of my daydream and traveled upstairs to bed.

Peace.

The next morning, the sun peaked its eyes into my bedroom at 8:05. Today was Sunday and I had the day off. I took the train into the city and walked across the National Lawn, there was ice skating and pretzel sells as usual. I ventured over to the Capitol Building where I saw a larger group gathering and yelling. As I got closer, their chants became more disassociated and fiercer. They were not in unison. In fact, the whole of them together sounded like an angry hornet nest, buzzing wildly through the quiet, cool February stillness.

Most of the men were wearing decorate coats and jackets with small bright, speckles on them. Military speckles. They were shouting things to each other and to passerby's. Two of the men ran up to me as quick as I stepped on the pavement in front of them.

"Sir," said a 30-something alpha-male, "Would you be interested in joining the armed forces?"

"What? Oh, er, no." I fought for a solid sentence. It wasn't often that *pro*-military groups were hunkered on the lawn. I had gotten so used to crying mothers hopelessly fighting for their son's untimely death. "No, I don't think so." It was almost a question.

A smaller, more wrinkled man started. "Son, joining the military is the best opportunity in the world for a young person like yourself. You can see the world, build a good resume, pay for college."

I was becoming more intrigued. I had indeed thought about the military when I came out of high school, but my parents were in my ears at the first thought of enlisting. They threw anti-war books in my direction, hit me with newspaper articles, and weekly communicated facts of death tolls and soldier life; two of the same to them.

They were long out of my head now, and the opportunity still looked worth the pitch.

"Go on," I beckoned.

The two men told me about the enlistment process, the 3 year requirement, the benefits, and even the downfalls. They made the downfalls seem simple to bear.

"You will have to push yourself to physical and emotional limits that most men your age can't endure. This job is not for everybody, but the one's who come out of it, are better men."

The younger man gave a nod like he was saying "Here, here!"

There was too much information running through my head. I could feel pressure from all sides closing in and forcing my mouth to make a final decision. War was cold, but honor was warm. Blood was dark, but sweat was a symbol of power. The truth was clear, I was in a large rut in my life, and I needed an escape clause. Before my mouth produced a verdict, new evidence was produced by the 30-something.

"Plus, you never know. You might grow up to save the world in the Army. What other job can you do that?" It almost looked like he winked at me, like he knew. A psychic, a missionary from Satin, or just a very good salesman, it didn't matter now. He had convinced the jury.

The first words to come out of my mouth in the last few minutes were, "Where do I sign?"

I returned on the subway that night a changed man, a better man. Every time I felt I had made a rash decision, there were 15 smart ideas to justify it. I slumped into my chair and thumbed through the flyers of elite, military gurus and killing-machines. I saw myself in their boots and their camouflage. I saw myself in their war paint and holding their rifles. I turned to the last page to a picture of Arlington National Cemetery.

I stopped. I had my parents in my ear. "This is where boys are buried. This is where the government puts you when your time in the Army is up. No party. No flowers. Just a plot of dirt and a little cement fixture."

That night I prayed. It was the first time in 3 years or so, but it was necessary. At first I was dumbfounded, didn't know what to say or how to say it. I kept trying though. If I got stuck, I would recite a Hail Mary or two that I learned from my grandma. That would give me the strength to say, "Forgive me, Lord" or "I need your help, God". Eventually, smooth verbiage flowed out of my mouth and I was Moses on the mount. My daydreaming was seeping into my prayers and making my speech became an awakening, a resurrection.

I was now fearless. Not a good state of mind for sleep.

8

The first church I went to was very wooden and very dim. I was 9 years old and I was with my grandmother. The church smelled like a novelty shop but had stained glass up the walls instead of trinkets. The church also reminded me of a store because my grandmother had to keep saying, "Don't touch anything." I wanted to very badly. It all seemed too fake to be real. Some of the Bibles were coverless in the pews from years of use and torture. My grandmother sat down next to me and squawked with the old lady in the pew ahead of us.

"Well good morning Jeanne," the old lady clucked, "I see you brought a cute, little thing with you today. He looks just like his grandfather."

"That he does. I'm trying to bring this one into the church life before he gets too old and becomes a grump like his grandfather too," replied my grandmother.

"Amen to that, Jeanne."

The preacher was very sweaty and bald. I didn't like him. He wasn't like my grandfather who was strapping and brave. Up at the podium, he looked nervous and excited all at once. He read from Matthew as if it were his own work. When he finished, I didn't know if I were to clap or sit still. I sat still.

The air was very stale in the church. The choir was slumped. It was not the grandeur that my grandmother made it seem, more like the paleness my grandfather hinted at. The preacher continued on about giving and receiving, receiving and giving, and Lord knows what else. I stared off at a candle in the corner when something in the sermon caught my attention.

The preacher boldly boomed to the pews, "...and the water was turned into wine!"

What?! I thought. *Jesus was a magician!* I indeed liked magicians. I even once wrote a note to my teacher saying this much and she thought I should do some more math problems. I tapped my grandmother on the hip. "Grandma, how did he do that trick?"

She smiled and said, "Oh, it was no trick Frankie. That's called having faith."

I went home that night and had so many fabulous daydreams in my chair. I had a new, brave word, 'faith'. I told my parents about church and they grinned and didn't hoist an opinion either way. I found out later their more personal reasons for not going to church so I never brought up the "f" word around them again.

My grandmother took me to church once a month for the next few years until she died of oldness. My mom told me not to call it that, but that's what it was, oldness. When my grandmother passed, I stopped going to church because my grandpa was a grump and I couldn't ask my parents.

Not until I was 14 did I enter back through a set of holy doors. These doors were also wooden, but the inside was a little less dim. The preacher was bright and young. There were a lot of girls at this church. I thought it was rude to notice them in church so I sat still some more. I concentrated on the words of the preacher. I was old enough now to understand that Jesus couldn't do magic, per say, but had more of an understanding for the "hows" in life.

"Jesus, *how* are we going to feed all these people?"

"An unlimited supply of bread and fish, duh," said Jesus. And it was done.

"Your holiness, *how* are we granted access to the kingdom of heaven?"

Jesus thought a little harder. "Don't be an ass."

The man whispered to his wife, "Does he mean like a donkey?" His wife responded, "No, not like a donkey, you ass." And it was done.

Finally a man asked Jesus, "Your most on-high-ly-ness-es." It was a little forced but Jesus bought it. "*How* are the Cubs ever going to win a World Series?" Jesus looked at the man and said, "Good sir, even I, the Son of Man, cannot help you on this one." And it was done.

What I learned in church at 14 wasn't a great impact to my spirituality, but it kept me out of trouble. True, I did daydream in church, but who's to say if that was a sin or not. By the time I was 16, I had picked up enough tidbits to practically write my own Bible. Don't kill anybody. Don't do anything stupid, and by stupid, I mean on purpose. Don't be angry at other people for being stupid. And don't swear, unless you play baseball or are writing a book.

These facts ruled my existence since my teenage years and followed me to this day. It was pretty simple.

"That kid asked if I wanted a beer but I'm only 17." *Don't do anything stupid.*

"Darn. I forgot to pay for this piece of delicious Twizzler that fell into my grocery bag." *Its okay, it wasn't on purpose.*

"Drat! I just failed my math test again, can I curse at it?" *Did you take your math test on a baseball field?* "No." *Are you wearing a jockstrap?* "No." *Then, no. You cannot swear.* "Dagburnit."

When I was 17, Angela took me to her church. She was southern Baptist and I couldn't sing very well. I was doomed from the beginning. Every time the chorus sang "Ohhhhhh" I sang "   ," but I mouthed the words so it looked like I was singing. In fact, I must have been good at it, because once an older lady in front of me told me after Hymnal 187 that I had a marvelous voice. I said "thank you" and when she turned back around I saw a marvelous hearing aid in her ear that was marvelously turned off. Still, a complement was a complement.

For most of my teenage life, church was a haven for me. It kept me humble, it kept me peaceful, and it kept me happy. Mark, Matthew, Luke and John had become alternative friends when Tom was at space camp and Angela was "girly". I fell into the pages of the Bible like a bird learning to fly. There was an awkward jump and then *splat*, the ground. I read pages at random because concentrating on one section too long made me antsy.

Most people would think this method is demeaning to a book, especially one of such grandeur. But I thought the contrary. I felt that if this book was written by the Lord himself, then I should be able to flip to any page and be enlightened with pureness and wisdom. It was true, and it made the story of Jesus that much more interesting.

Matthew 2:1 - Mary accidentally births the Son of God.

Luke 9:13 – Who, indecently, was a heck of a water skier.

Genesis 1:1 – But then, who wouldn't be a great athlete coming from such a promising gene pool?

Job 1:13 – Well, probably not Job, because let's face it, he doesn't have the best of luck.

Ecclesiastes 9:12 – Although, this dude says luck happens to everyone. Ironically, his luck was winning the National Spelling Bee by correctly spelling his own name.

John 20:6 – But the name "Jesus" was made permanent for all people, throughout time, when he pulled the biggest stunt of all time. The Empty Tomb.

I loved hearing different preachers tell the story of the empty tomb. My favorite was a preacher by the name of Rev. Dan at the Baptist church. Rev. Dan had a knack to yell with a Southern draw and pound the podium when he spoke.

"And Mary went to the tomb of the Lord Jesus." *Pound.* "And the <u>disciples</u> went to the tomb of <u>your</u> Lord Jesus." *Pound.* "There was nothing but strips of linen!" *Pound pound.* "The guards rushed to the tomb and were in awe, complete stillness. They had put Jesus' body there themselves. They had held his flesh and placed him in the coffin and placed the coffin in the tomb and stood there, watching." *Pound.* "He had been dead. He was lifeless. He was nothing." *Pound.* "Jesus, our king, our savior, had made something out of nothing." *Pound.*

This is why I went to church. The ultimate story, the ultimate plot, the ultimate ending. I was beginning to understand life, why it worked the way it did. I was beginning to understand what my life was about, its purpose, its qualities to offer. It was beyond simple.

Live like Jesus. He was the perfect character and his life was the perfect story. So I tried. I did what I could with not what I had, and I felt good. This theory came to a standstill later that year.

Rev. Dan and I became very good friends and we had a meeting every Wednesday about God. I would ask questions about life and he would tell me to ask God. I would ask him a question about death and he would tell me to ask God. Rev. Dan was a good man and I took his advice.

"God," I would say at night, "what's heaven like?"

God thought for a long second. "Well, I can't really explain it, only you can."

"Pardon."

"Yes, see, heaven is what ever you think it should be; whatever will make you most happy and content. It's different for everybody, of course. When you die you have as long in heaven as you want. You can look at photographs you never took, movies of yourself you never filmed, and any question you have about anything will be answered. Simple as that. And when you've seen all your movies and answered all your questions, and heaven is no longer a place where you want to be. It ends." God snapped his fingers. "Just like that."

God and I had talks every once in a while. I would tell Dan what God told me and together we made a list of truths. These truths were what I called "my purpose" and what Rev. Dan called "my next sermon". Together, the three of us learned.

Rev. Dan died on November 21st. A very, very cold night. He was hit by a drunk driver. And so it goes.

I lost my religion then. I lost my faith then. I cried out to a sick, tormented God. "What did he ever do to you!?" I screamed. "He was perfectly fine here on earth. He went to church because he loved *you*. For crying out loud, he *was* the church!" I was getting frustrated. "Why didn't you take me? I go to church for the stories, the drama, the hope that one day I'll listen to a preacher and Jesus *will* be in that tomb. Yeah. I want, just once, for Jesus to be lying there, cold, helpless, dead. The way Rev. Dan is now. That's how it should be. That's how it really happens!"

God knew this was not a time to talk back. He turned his head and walked out of my room. We both knew he was right, but it was no use. Neither of us wanted to fight anymore. All of the things God had taught me had gone out the window. His wisdom was useless to me now.

I realized later, the time of my life that I spent with Rev. Dan and God, I was already happy and content. Anything He said to me, I would just accept, no doubts. I had no pain in my life.

When Rev. Dan died, I fell out of my comfort zone. I felt pain. God had been wrong about too many things and I wanted Him to vanish.

There's always a catch. God's catch was that everything dies sometime. It was a very good catch. And that is why I returned to my knees the night I signed up for the Army. I was helpless and we both knew it, God and me. When I started to pray, I felt God creep back into my room. Before I went to bed, I asked Him, "God, I'm going to be alright in the Army aren't I?"

"Of course Frank. You had your dream didn't you? Did that look like you were in the Army?

I was half surprised. "Y-you know about my dreams?"

"Please don't mock me. Plus, I'll do one better than your dreams, since it's a nice night and I'm feeling generous. I'll *guarantee* that you will not die in the Army. How about that?"

"Thanks God, I needed that. Oh, and sorry for not talking to you in the last few years. It's kinda been, well..."

God put a hand up. I knew what he meant and He smiled as He walked out of my room. We would talk another time.

9

I've been in the Army for 561 days. I keep a count on the edges of my pages. The sand outside lies still and hot underneath a beautifully lit sky. The stars here in Saudi Arabia are jewels. I think of Aladdin at every dune and even dig through a few inches of sand searching for a lamp when the Captain isn't looking. I know I will never find one, but it keeps me alive, gives me a purpose. Most the soldiers walk around like zombies thriving on pure instinct, blood, and fear. They speak of sex and killing like they were games that earn points for each score. Fights break out daily and more then often they involve me. I have become a token amongst the brutes. They are afraid of me because I am different than them, because I write and read and care about the people I am shooting at. But at the same time, they respect me. I might have been involved in many fights, but I also have won the majority of them. Most importantly, the other brutes are jealous of my rifling. One of the corporals said I shot like a girl the other day. So I put two quick pops inside of his two on a target from 100 meters. He must have thought I was being cocky and took a swing at my forehead. I duck and broke his nose with my forearm. So it goes.

Through all of the agony and dullness of the day, I still love the night, with the stars and the cool. It reminds me of D.C. and the day I left home. It was 561 days ago.

The morning before I left, I slept in for the first time in months. It was good. Tom called me at 10 and wanted to know if I could go to lunch with him and some friends. One friend was Gina and the other was the Tambourine. We went to our favorite Chinese restaurant.

At the restaurant, I told Tom about leaving for the army. He didn't seem to like the idea, but knew it was what I wanted. He helped me pack up my stuff that evening before the party. We gently tripped over memories of our childhood found in comic books and photographs I had stored in boxes in my closets. Gina drove by at seven to pick us up.

As I left the house, I looked back at a long day of cleaning, thinking, and laughing; one I surely would never forget. On the way out the door, I grabbed my keys, wallet, and a blank notepad. That night at the party, I wrote the first chapter of my novel.

The next morning was not so innocent. I awoke to my alarm clock honking wildly in my direction. *Bahn... bahn... bahn!* I remember the morning being colder than most mornings because there was a corner of frost on my window which was very uncommon for April. I snapped off the clock. My shower and breakfast were quiet and nervous. I grabbed my yellow duffel of clothes and locked the door behind me.

The post where I was to meet up with my fellow new recruits was next to a secondhand shoe store in the west end. When I pulled up, there was a faded black jeep with US Army paraphernalia on the back windshield. A recruiting officer I had met before stepped out in a very straight uniform. I could guess he thoroughly enjoyed the days when he got to wear it. I turned off the ignition and the smoke oozing out of my maroon station wagon was snipped. I approached and saluted the man.

"Welcome cadet." He boomed and returned a salute. "It's a big day isn't it?"

"Yessir," I said. "I'm very excited, sir."

"Good."

Silence. There was not much to talk about between a to-be-cadet and his to-be-officer. We had not yet been thrown into a position where he would do the yelling and

I would do the running. We also were past a position where he did the recruiting and I did the listening. We were very awkward. We stood and looked at the ground and stood and looked at his paraphernalia and stood and breathed cold air.

Another car showed up. A mother in a midnight blue Cadillac pulled in with her son. The son had a buzzed head and stern grin and the mother was almost in tears - correct that - definitely in tears when she moved around the hood of the Caddy to embrace her son. The woman was large and Hispanic and took a while to get around the hood, but when she did, it was Niagara Falls. The son, still stern, gave a one armed squeeze and marched in our direction. After the car chugged off, the boy gave us a salute and a name.

"Sir," saluting at the Sir, "honor to be here, sir."

"Likewise," replied the Sir.

The boy turned to me with an outstretched hand. "Jesus Menendez."

I grabbed his hand and offered my name. He returned to the Sir with comments on the unusual weather and admiration for the Sir's outfit. I couldn't help but giggle with a joke I just made. Tom was always wondering what Catholics thought of the war, and now I could tell him, "They think it's great, in fact, their leader is in my training squad."

Two more boys showed up in equally solemn situations as Jesus. They were Hispanic, shaved, and presented a firm grip. The four of us climbed into the back of the Sir's Jeep and we were off. I was entering the world of warfare.

The first stop in the world of warfare was at a Quickie Mart of Route 31. The Sir needed to pick up a puck of chewing tobacco. It was a speed bump in my road of expectations, but I guess it was somewhat necessary. We again were off.

Twenty miles further, the Sir had a craving for a chilidog and an urge to talk to the cute female clerk there. I think he had dated her once because she seemed like she was yelling – correct that – definitely yelling at him through the window of the gas station kiosk. *Ah, army life, so many infidels, so little time.*

Around 9 am, we finally drove through the gates of Camp Belmont, a rural military base northwest of D.C. Camp Belmont was less of a base and more of just space; lots of empty space. There was over grown fields clawing at the road as we drove in. There was a gas station and two cabins over looking an empty parking lot.

"There's the helicopter pad," informed the Sir.

Indeed the helicopter pad was a former parking lot, but I wasn't one to question the authority on my first day. Sir took us to our barracks and gave us a stack of papers.

"Fill these out, take a look around the place, get to know the other soldiers. We meet up at Mess at 1200 hours." A salute and back to the Jeep.

There were a few others meandering around the barracks, but no one really talked. The sounds were mostly just bags unzipping and the occasional introductions.

"How's it going?" I asked the soldier next to my bunk.

"Good enough," he said. "Tomorrow is going to suck though."

"Why's that?"

"PT."

He was right. Tomorrow did suck. The Sir was at the drill field very early and already had started on his chew. The morning wasn't too bad, just constant running. I was fairly good at running in that I could do it for a long time, but got bored after a while. The afternoon was a little worse. The Sir had us doing, what I called, "stupid shit". He would tell us an uncomfortable position to be in, say, standing on one leg with an index finger on our noses, and we were to remain in that position for an ungodly amount of time. After the pose, we would drop down to pushups or sit-ups or a combination of the two.

The reason I called this "stupid shit" was because of how everybody looked around me when we were doing this; stupid. I remember one position in particular. Sir called it the "cockroach". We lay supine on the dirt with legs and arms straight towards the sky. Sir would periodically go around to each soldier and put 20 pound weights in his hands. After a few minutes the weights would shift to another soldier and so on. This went on for an hour and 15 minutes. The grunts and screams of soldiers started at 30 minutes into the routine but faded out to pure numbness by 50 minutes.

Sir walked and chewed, walked and chewed. If a soldier had the misfortune of dropping a weight or losing his balance and toppling over, Sir would send a boot into the soldier's side. I dropped the weights twice.

Pug! The Sir's boot pummeled my rib cage and I quickly picked up the weights in a coughing fit. Again 40 minutes later. *Pug!* Another boot in the ribs. Same spot. The Sir had a good memory.

After our session of being statues, we returned to the Mess Hall for slop and then back to the fields for more running. At night we fought. We always fought. The Sir had a ring painted on the helicopter parking lot and this was *where* we fought. We had old boxing gloves with only a quarter inch of padding to strike with and this is *how* we fought.

The rules were simple. One - if you stepped out of the ring before the fight was over, Sir got 30 seconds in the ring with you. Two - if you got knocked down or knocked out, you had to fight an extra fight that night. Three - everybody had to fight three times a night, for five minutes, no exceptions. If the fight was not good enough, we had to fight Sir. And so we fought.

I had only punched another human once in my life, I was eleven, and she was twelve. I had a feeling this was going to be different.

My first fight was against a smaller Hispanic named Julio. He was short, but much quicker than I suspected, he came at me quick with 5 hard jabs into my rib cage. He must have had a good memory too. I bellowed in pain and unleashed a shot to his left eye. Julio dropped in a lump on the pavement. It was over.

My next fight was not as easy. I faced a shaved boy named Ewing. We lasted all 5 minutes and shared equally blue cheek bones at the end of it.

The last fight of the night was between me and a larger boy named Mike D. I'm not sure what the D stood for, but we always called him Mike D. His last name was Smith. Mike D opened the round with a heavy blow in my stomach. I curled up and softened two more to the chest. I finally connected in his jaw and ribs in two subsequent punches and Mike D backed off. He wiped the sweat from his eyes and again stepped towards me. He missed a large swing at my ear and I connected again with an uppercut that sent him spinning. He stumbled under his own weight and fell to the ground. It was over. I stepped over to Mike D and helped him to his feet.

"Foul!" cried Sir.

"What?" I said when I realized he was looking at me.

"Foul, cadet! You stepped out of the ring before the fight was over, you've got 30 seconds with me, boy."

I had been shafted. "Sir, the fight was over. Mike was down."

"He was down, but not out. Get in the ring!"

I did. The next thirty seconds was too quick to handle. Sir didn't hesitate continuing where his boot left off, ramming me a dozen times or more in the side. Then, he brought a final blow when I wasn't looking. Plap! My chin arched back and I mimicked a toppling stack of bricks.

Sir waited 10 seconds and then dragged my limp body out of the ring. "Mike, Julio, you've got one more fight. I want it now!"

I laid in bed that night on my right side because my left was purple. The next day was not so much different than the first. There was running, there was posing, there was fighting, in that order. And the day after that was also similar. And after that, and so on. Whenever I wanted to quit, the Sir had a catchphrase that would keep me there, in hell.

"What cadet? Do you miss your mom? I bet you wish you were home with her right now, eating her pancakes and watching TV? You make me sick. Give me another twenty!"

Before I could get out a "No, Sir!" it was back to pushups in the dirt. Down. Dirt. Up. Spit. Down. Dirt. Up. Spit. And it continued this way. After two weeks, the dirt lost its taste. It became a part of our diet just like the stale macaroni and old potatoes in the Mess Hall. My bruises would eventually heal only to be replaced by new ones. I would sweat in the day, pant in the night, and toss in my sleep. The day before I left Camp Belmont I regained my dignity.

"C'mon you son-of-a-bitch!" These were the words of the boy I was about to fight. He was angry and confused and took two swings at my head. I had become the best fighter at camp and everybody wanted a piece of me.

"Is that all you've got!" The boy was fighting with anger, something I could never understand. I learned to fight with poise and intelligence over the two week period and it paid off. I had beaten larger opponents and faster opponents, and this one was no different. I ducked from another punch and drilled a shot to the boy's chest. He fell down in heavy breathing that he couldn't catch. I watched him sit there on his knees for five seconds when I had a brilliant idea. I stepped out of the ring.

"Foul!" cried Sir.

"Oops," I said.

"Oh, I've been waiting for this one cadet."

"As have I, Sir."

The Sir stepped into the ring and charged with pure adrenaline. He centered on my rib cage again but was denied by my biceps held tight against my body. He backed away. This time, I enclosed on him. I held my hands just below my eye level and peered at my weaker target. Each time I threw a blow, my mouth would let out a "phoo" of air. Jab, jab. Hook. Jab. I backed up and took a breath. Sir looked scared. He charged at me a final time with only fear and anxiety. I caught him in the mouth before he could even throw his first punch. Sir fell harder than all of the boys at the camp that week. When his body hit the pavement, a few cadets ran to help him to his feet and he pushed them away.

He propped his body up with his elbows and took a deep breath. "Well done, cadet." A quick salute and he disappeared in to the night. That was the last time I ever saw Sir. It was done.

After Basic Training, I and a few other cadets from my troop were sent to a base just outside of Charleston, South Carolina. Charleston had beautiful beaches, palm trees, perfect sunshine everyday, and Drill Sergeant

O'Neal. Sergeant was not near as young as Sir. He had wrinkles falling down his face under his aviator glasses. I never saw the man's eyes, just mine, looking back at me through the lenses. He wore his pants very high and always had a white t-shirt tucked into them with shiny dog tags around his neck. He did not have the same pride in a uniform like Sir. He knew his job very well; make us killing machines.

If we were lazy, he would work us until we threw up. If we were cocky, he'd put us in our place. If we were good, he'd reward us with a couple hours of down time, and then work us again for being too lazy. This was our schedule.

My favorite part about Sergeant was he focused less on beating the shit out of soldiers and more on tactics. The first day on base, he told us his philosophy. "I don't give a shit if you can do any of that karate nonsense or even if you have a decent right hook. In war, you have to do two things, run and shoot. You run to a spot where you are hidden and then you shoot your enemy. It is not difficult, gentlemen. But, if you miss your target when you shoot, you will die. But then again, if you can't shoot a goddamn stationary target, you might as well de-list and run home to your momma right now!"

Sergeant had a way with words.

After a couple of miles in dead sprint with my fellow soldiers, we fell into rank at the edge of a shooting range. Sergeant pulled up on a golf cart carrying a large rifle.

"This, gentlemen, is a M16 active combat rifle. This is going to be your best friend and greatest enemy for the next few weeks. When you leave here and enter full, active duty, you will be issued this gun. Has anyone ever shot a rifle before?"

I was hesitant to raise my hand. A few other soldiers raised theirs proudly and I decided to be honest and extend mine.

"Soldier, step forward."

Shit. That soldier was me.

I walked toward Sergeant and took the extended gun from his hand.

"Take a shot at that target down there son." His eyes were fierce, or mine were, it was hard to tell with his glasses on. I cocked the rifle and took aim at the target far in the distance. I fired once. Perfect.

The sergeant was slightly impressed. "Good shot, son. I've never had anyone hit the bull on the first try. Where'd you learn to shoot?"

"Sir, I shot my grandfather's rifle when I 14, sir."

I could feel Sergeant's eyes get fiercer while mine stayed the same. "Don't fuck with me, son! Now I've only seen a few men in my lifetime shoot a gun better than that, so either call beginner's luck or tell me the truth!"

I sighed. "It was beginner's luck sir. I'm not that good of a shot."

"Bullshit! Shoot it again!"

I knew whatever the outcome of this episode with Sergeant, it would mean Hell to pay for the next few weeks. Three hours on base and I had already managed to tick off the head honcho. *I should have kept my hand down.*

Through my scope were the bull's eye and the hole where my first bullet went through. I thought about shooting my second bullet through that same hole but wisely decided that might be too cocky. I took my second shot right above the first making a tangent intersection between the two holes, like a figure eight.

"Goddamn it soldier! You just cost your platoon the reward of running for the rest of the afternoon." Sighs came from all around. "Take off!"

A small assistant of the Sergeant's led us on our runs. His name was Lenny and he was short and energetic. He made sure we kept pace and kept our mouths closed on long runs where Sergeant couldn't watch us. Lenny and I were in the front of the line.

"Kid," Lenny said, "Why didn't you just tell him where you learned to shoot, he wouldn't have cared."

"I was telling the truth, sir, I haven't shot a rifle in almost 8 years."

Lenny was looking at my face for a tell or a bluff. I was sincere. "Well, you keep shooting like that, and you'll be out of this dump soon enough." For the rest of the run, I thought about Lenny's point.

When we got back to the barracks that night, four soldiers were angrily waiting my arrival.

A fatter one started, "Yo! You think you're hot shit out there, sucking up to the Sergeant with a couple good shots, huh?"

Another piped in, "Yeah, you think you're better than us?"

"No." I pleaded.

"Of course you ain't."

79

The fatter one stepped forward. "Nope." He swung a hard fist at my face and landed at a spot between my eye and my mouth. I thought for a moment about the irony of leaving my last camp for this one. I blacked out.

The next morning we returned to the shooting range. Sergeant had a full rack of guns to make sure everyone got a fair turn. For the first hour, a retired Navy sharpshooter gave us specific details on how to assemble, clean, shoot, disassemble, and even carry a gun. It was not informative for me. After the speech, we were siphoned into our designated shooting booths and instructed to take ten shots. I thought about the different ways to irritate Sergeant today. I put ten shots in the middle of the target all within a centimeter of each other so that there was just a half inch diameter circle torn from the bull's eye when I was finished.

Sergeant came to my booth and took a look at the target from a distance. "Well, it looks like beginner's luck indeed soldier," he started with a laugh. "Only one shot on the whole goddam target." He didn't understand.

I started to reel in the paper and said, "No, sir. I shot all ten bullets inside the same hole sir." Sure enough, as the paper got closer, Sergeant's mouth got sicker. The paper stopped on the line in front of us, I grabbed it, and handed it to Sergeant. "Ten shots sir, you can check my barrel if you'd like."

"N-no son. Good work. Um. Good work." And he walked away to the next booth.

Lenny was very right about a lot of things. And I was ordered to active duty after 4 days.

Sergeant came into our barracks at an odd hour and summoned me with an extended index finger. I shuffled back to his office and sat in the hard chair he was pointing to.

"Son, I've never seen a shooter like you in all the years I've been in the military. I've ordered an immediate withdrawal for you from training duty to full, active duty. You will leave tomorrow at 1200 hours. There's a colonel that is eager to meet you and get you on the first plane to the Middle East. There's a rifle group there, Rifle Company Thirteen. They are the best shots in the military as far as I'm concerned. I've put in a good word and I think you won't be hassled too much after they see you shoot. Good luck soldier." And with that, another salute.

I didn't know what to think. So I didn't. The military taught me that. Whenever you find a situation in which you can choose right or wrong, don't, let someone else choose it for you.

I packed my bags and left the next day at noon. I was on a plane directed east that night and arrived in a barren wasteland at 10 am the next day. The sand was rolling when I hopped off the plane. The eager colonel shielded his eyes from the storm and ran towards me, yelling over the noise of the plane.

"Welcome to Saudi Arabia, soldier!" he saluted. "I've heard a lot about you. Doesn't miss a target, they say! Well, this is the place for you, son!"

We climbed into his Jeep and jetted off down a twenty miles stretch of sand and rock and orange. He asked questions about my training and I responded with yes or no answers.

We finally arrived at a collage of tents and vehicles, all colored tan. Soldiers were performing their PT for the day and I was instructed to put away my bags and join them as soon as possible. I caught up with the group on their run.

"Company halt!" barked a superior officer. "Soldiers, this is a new recruit, he will be joining us for the remainder of our tour. This is his first tour, so please get him up-to-date as quickly as possible." A salute and then back to the sand.

These soldiers were a little less juvenile then the cadets in the states, yet they were more dangerous and hurtful when they did happen to become juvenile. That night I was inducted by the soldiers with a new tattoo and another fight. The tattoo was a burnt on number thirteen and the fight left me badly bruised. The next morning I got to shoot.

Phap! Phap! Two perfect strikes went through a target at 80 meters. Colonel was impressed. I learned from the other soldiers about the situation in which we were assigned. One soldier in particular put it the best. "We kind of just hang out all day. Then we shoot some people when we get a call. And then we hang out some more."

Simple enough.

This day was a hanging out day. Tomorrow was a killing day.

We got a call at 0900 hours and Colonel rounded us up. "We've got a small party of Saudis two kilometers west with heavy artillery. Navy is afraid of them advancing closer to port and needs us to wipe them out before anything can happen."

We set off in the Humvees, kicking dirt behind us for miles. Just before a large dune we stopped and unloaded. Colonel instructed me to follow another soldier up to the edge. We gazed down at a dozen or more dark-skinned Saudis carrying two trucks worth of homemade missiles. They were eating lunch.

Colonel snuck up behind me and took a look for himself. "Easy," he said, "Let's let Frank here take 'em out. He needs a kill or two under his belt."

"Alright," said the soldier I had followed.

There were three of us on the ridge of the sand dune. We focused in on our targets and thought quickly in our mind the best way to skip from man to man. After a few moments of planning, Colonel said, "On my command." He took a final look through his binoculars and calmly said, "Fire."

I did. So did the others. I shot four times and killed four Saudis instantly. It was easy, but odd. When the last Saudi fell, I cocked my head with a slight bit of unease. I thought to myself that the man I had just killed looked like a mouse would if you put it in the microwave. It felt strange but simplistic.

The soldier to my left had only clipped a man in his abdomen. The man's body was wriggling on the ground like a worm. I took aim and put him out of his misery. The other soldier turned to me offended.

"Why'd you do that?"

"I didn't want him to suffer," I suggested.

"Are you saying I can't shoot?" accused the soldier.

I didn't say anything. I would get punched in the face later that night for my actions.

Colonel separated the other soldier and turned to me. "Good work, Frank. Let's move out, everyone!"

I looked out the rear of the Humvee on the ride back to camp. The sand splashed from the tires like tiny ocean waves. I tried to remember life four weeks earlier, just before I had left, before I had killed a man. I could not.

10

Every night during my first 6 months of active duty, I wrote. It was the only thing to keep me civilized. Mostly, I wrote this book, but there were others - letters to Tom, poems about home, essays about the war – stuff like that. Like I said, it kept me civilized, but it did not keep me safe. Most of the men at the camp already thought I was weaker than them, so when I took out a pen and paper, the stereotype was hardened.

They looked at my twig arms and my long body and saw a man not fit for killing. The irony was, with a rifle, I was the best killer they had. Colonel started sending me on scout missions with the first battalion after only a month. He told me every time he saw me, what a fortunate position I was in to move up in rank so fast. "Dammit Frank, I've never given anyone the privilege of being a first brigade sniper after only a month, but you've earned it. What are you up to now, thirty kills? Forty?"

"Forty six sir."

"Forty six kills. Whew. And how many shots do you think you have fired, son?"

"Forty six sir. It took me two shots to hit a man crouched behind a tire last week. But, I made up for it later that day when I hit another man in the chest and it ricocheted through his brother's head. It was a lucky shot sir."

"Forty six shots. Huh." And Colonel was off.

I met up with the other snipers at the shooting range. The shooting range at our camp was very simple. We'd get a newly recruited Marine from the next camp over and have him drive a half-dead Humvee out until we said "Stop!" on the radio.   Then the marine would run back to where we were shooting from before we started firing at the target on the back of the Humvee. If we demolished the target or needed more distance on the Humvee, the Marine was ready in full hustle.

My first day on the range, I was assigned a scout. His name was Leonard Banks but everyone called him Goose (like that was any better). Goose was a 25 year old private with no common sense what-so-ever, but was a complete Almanac of military boggle. He saluted me when he arrived and was even quicker to shake my hand. Goose was a soggy fellow with red hair and pasty skin. He appeared very happy and even glowing when he approached me.

"It's an honor to meet you Frank. The word back home is that you're the best shooter in the stink right now."

The other snipers stopped assembling their guns and turned to this boastful punk. Most of the snipers were older than Goose which made them even older than me. The last thing I wanted was another group of soldiers ready and willing to abuse me.

I tried to calm Goose down. "Well I haven't really shot that much yet Goose so I don't think I'm nearly as good as some of these guys." I lied through my teeth loud enough so that the others would hear it and gave Goose a wink. He seemed to have caught my drift and changed the subject to the business at hand.

"Well, let me see your gun here. A standard M-40, just like my dad had."

"Your dad was in the Marines?"

"Sure was. He was a scout for 15 years and I plan on doing the same."

I liked his enthusiasm, but again it seemed to irritate the other gunners to my left.

"Hey Goose, what d'ya say we stick to shooting for now and talk later," I said to cool the mood.

"Of course Frank. I've already got your spot. Two clicks east, not much wind today.

I took aim at the Humvee. Without a scope, the Humvee was too far away to even try to squint at. But magnified, I was back in my comfort zone. Pop. Pop. Two perfect shots through the circle. The other scouts, who were still trying to get a fix on the wind, saw my shots through their binoculars and lost all concentration.

"Did you see that?" I overheard one scout say to his sniper.

"So what. Beginner's luck."

I waited patiently for the rest of the snipers to finish their shots and then watched as the Marine took off in a dead heat towards the Humvee. The 1st Team sniper was in charge of the walkie-talkie and had the Marine move the car out to 200 meters (the maximum standard range for the M-40). When the Marine finished his sprint Goose's voice was in my head.

"Er. Three clicks east. Er. Watch the head wind Frank; maybe take it up a little." Goose was right again. A perfect shot.

The snipers were getting jealous. It took most of them 5 shots to even hit the target. I watched the Marine giggle quietly to himself and then stop suddenly when the 1st Team sniper walked up behind me.

"What's your name again?" were the words I heard shout thorugh the back of my head. The soldier wasn't loud, he just approached so quietly on the sand that any noise at all besides gun fire came as a shock. His deep bass rattled my spine and made me gulp, but I composed myself and managed to let out a "F-Frank, sir".

"Don't call me sir, Frank." He wasn't angry, but far from cheerful as well. "Where'd you learn to shoot, Frank?"

Uh oh. I had been in that unwelcoming position before. I lied. "The army s-." I was about to say sir again but held it.

"Ha," said the soldier while looking at his scout for a second laugh. "The army, he says. Well, good shooting soldier. If you keep practicing, you might be able to hit more than just that Humvee some day." The soldier turned to walk away. The conversation was done. I couldn't tell if he had complimented me or insulted me, but I didn't care. Goose took it as an insult.

"Maybe you should be practicing. He out-shot you didn't he?" Goose was just elected my spokesperson without my consent and now we were both in for a fight.

"Excuse me!" Now the soldier was definitely angry. "I hit the target too you little shit. Just because your boy here got lucky on his first two doesn't mean anything!"

"I bet he can hit from 300 meters," said Goose as if I was now his prized pig at the county fair.

"Bullshit. That gun only can fly 200-250 with a tailwind. You're loony. Ha! Are you guys hearing this kid?" he turned to ask the larger group that was now interested in Goose's proposal.

The soldier and Goose continued with pointless bantering for a few odd minutes about who was a better shooter, which scout had an uglier mother, and the physics beyond a 300 yard shot. Finally the quarrels stopped when the soldier yelled, "Marine!"

The Marine's face molded from a pleasant contentment to utter gloom in a second. He already knew what words would come next. "Move the target to 300 meters!"

The entire time the soldier and Goose argued and the Humvee was moved, I had not spoken. Goose was speaking on my behalf and I couldn't complain. It was nice being appreciated for a change. After the vehicle was in place, the marine hopped out and began his long sprint back to the crowd. A challenge was worked out between Goose and the soldier in a type of shoot-off. I would get one shot to hit the target. If I missed, Goose would spend the night sleeping outside the nearest latrine for a week. If I hit, the soldier would get five shots to hit the target, otherwise he would be the unlucky sleeper.

A bigger crowd had formed and all eyes were on me and Goose as we reloaded the gun and hunkered into a shooting position on the sandy floor.

"Goose," I spoke close to a whisper, "Why would you do that? Do you know what the odds of me hitting this thing are?"

"Trust me Frank. You damned well know that I trust *you* right now." So he did. "Four clicks east now and, er," he stopped. "I would prop that bad boy up about 10 degrees."

"Ten degrees?" I broke my whisper. "That's insane Goose!"

"Trust me Frank. My dad taught me this one."

I didn't speak again and my eye honed in on the target. It was a marble in my scope; just a small sphere of color, but no real judge for distance. I checked my gun like Goose told me. *One, two, three, four clicks east. Ten degrees up.* My finger slid over the trigger and lightly pulled it in. Phap!

90

I didn't think I hit it at first, and listening to the sighs in the crowd, no one thought I did either. Then Goose broke in, "Right down the middle, again," he said as if it were going out of style.

"What!" the soldiers shouted, "Give me those!" The ripped the binoculars from his scout and gritted his teeth. Sure enough, I was the only one to the hit the inside, red circle that day, and now there were four gaping wounds through it, not three.

The crowd bustled. "Did you see that?"

"I've never even heard of a 300 meter shot before!"

"What'd he say his name was again?"

The soldier reluctantly kept his word and traded places with me and Goose. His first shot missed somewhere into space. I caught the second shot when it buried into the ground in front of the Humvee and spit sand in the air. The third and fourth shots again disappeared from the atmosphere. The soldiers fifth shot was the closest. I watched a spark dance off the silver bumper on the Humvee and a full second later the sound reached my ear. Ping!

The crowd applauded. The soldier thrashed his gear into the scout's arms and took off to his barracks. I was elated and Goose was grateful. "Nice shot Frank, he said sincerely. I asked him if he would consider being my fulltime scout. He smiled and agreed.

That night, while the defeated soldier was uncomfortably sleeping under a bright sky, unleveled sand, and the most atrocious stench in the Eastern Hemisphere, I had the best sleep of my life. After writing another chapter of my book, and a day that filled another chapter of my life, I thought about what I had accomplished as a soldier. I thought about the life I left behind in D.C. for the first time in months and I thought about my parents. I wondered if they knew what kind of man I had become.

11

I remember the night it happened. I was 8 years old and there was a storm outside my window. The rain was softly tapping the roof outside and making my eyes heavy. But, just as my eyelids started to slide - *Bang!* – another clap of thunder shook my bones. The lightning in the distance would flick light through the hallway bouncing off pictures of me and Italian paintings. On the streets I would hear fire engine wails screaming through the cool air. My body was frozen under the sheets and blanket on that cruel, cruel night. It was February 13th.

My parents were not there to comfort me that evening; they hardly ever were those days. That night, in particular, I knew exactly where they were, a banquet at the Archives Building downtown Washington. They were invited by a friend of theirs, Benny.

They left the house that night with my father in a rich tuxedo and my mother in a dazzling dress that would make Marilyn Monroe proud. They kissed me on the cheek as they smiled and waved goodbye. My mother's lipstick clung to my face as I desperately tried to rub it off. The sitter told me to hold still while she wiped the crimson residue off with a wet towel. After some time in my chair, I was ordered upstairs for a bath and bed. My sitter tucked me in my chilled sheets. She caught my fearful eyes staring out of the window. "Now don't worry about the storm Frankie. Just think about something happy, you'll have better dreams that way."

"I don't have dreams," I snapped.

"Fine. Then have a good sleep." She closed the door half way as she strolled downstairs.

I tried to sleep, but it didn't come. What did instead was a lightshow in my bedroom and random moments of heavy vibrations and the sound of a Timpani drum. I was scared. After an hour or more, the violent surges of nature seemed to calm themselves and collect into a random movement of noise. The rain and thunder held the same volume level and I was at peace again.

At 2:42, there was a boom. I flung my self upward and gasped. I knew it was 2:42 because the first image I saw was my alarm clock glaring red digital numbers at me. The clock had an evil grin. I grabbed my chest, more scared than earlier. The boom that woke me was from outside, or was it a dream? I looked out my window at something that was very much not a dream.

There, in the pitch of the night, a cloud of red and orange curling upward. It was in the direction of downtown. I yelled for my sitter who awoke from the downstairs couch and came clomping up the stairs.

"What is it Frankie? Did you have a nightm-," she held her breath and her feet stopped walking. When she came through the door, her eyes went from me to the window and froze her in time and place, as I was. We both sat and stared. We watched as the cloud rose higher and wider than our minds could conceive.

Both of us jumped when a quick rumbling of fighter jets flew over the house. My dad used to take me to air shows every other weekend in the summer and the pair of aircraft that flew over our house that night were easily recognizable as military-use. It seemed only like a split second for my sitter, but as the planes charged pass, I could feel their power, and their tone was familiar. F-18s.

The sitter rushed me downstairs when the red cloud grew darker and we turned on the television. The newscaster was holding back tears. "Two unidentified aircraft have just bombed a street corner in downtown Washington late this evening. We have no further word on if this was a terrorist plot or how many casualties there were. We will keep you updated as information arises." The screen went back to footage of a closer viewing of the red cloud and a caption reading "Bombing in the Capitol".

The sitter was more frantic than I was. I was probably too young at the time and still was confused as to what terrorism even meant. The sitter kept saying "Oh my God" and having a face like she was about to cry. She rushed to the telephone and I watched as she dialed my parents. "Let's see if your mom knows what's happening. Please pick up. Please pick up."

The sitter grew more pained when the voicemail answered and she stuttered through a message. "C-Call me and Frankie b-back soon, p-p-please." And then we sat.

I fell asleep on top of the sitter's leg and woke in the morning with a blanket over me and I was huddled on the couch. I opened my eyes weary of reality and the events that took place the night before. The TV was still on with a new caption. The sitter had moved to my daydreaming chair and she was sobbing uncontrollably now. I went back to the screen. The caption read, "Washington Monument and Archives Building destroyed in terrorist bombing."

I couldn't breathe. I kept looking back and forth from the TV to the sitter without any words to say. My world felt out of place and I cried hard.

My parent's death was confirmed at 6:00 that evening. I was about to eat a bowl of soup the sitter had fixed me when the phone rang and I waited. The sitter answered and immediately put a hand to her mouth. I didn't need to know anymore. I left my soup and ran up to my room. My mind was lost.

My grandparents moved into the house a few days later and became my official guardians when the papers went through. I didn't speak to them too much for a few months. I mostly just watched as my grandmother made me dinner and my grandfather watched golf on TV. This is when my best friend became the chair. It is where I could let go of reality and be someone else.

After a few weeks, I developed a bad habit of talking to my invisible parents. I would see my mom as if she were walking across the kitchen floor in new, leather sandals holding a tray of brownies. I would say, "Hey mom, are those for me and Tom."

"Not until after your dinner, young man."

"Ugh. Fine," I would whine.

My grandmother became particularly worried about my problem when she found out who I was talking to. I explained to her that I knew my parents were dead and that they were not in the house, but she still didn't seem at ease when I talked to them. I went to a psychiatrist about the problem. He would have sessions twice a week with me and my grandmother.

The psychiatrist was skinny and smelled like garlic. He would say, "Frank, you do know your mother and father are dead?"

"Yes."

"Then why do you keep talking to them?"

"Because, it makes me happy," I said confidently.

"Frank. I'm going to need you to stop talking to your parents. You have to be able to let go of your bond with them and move on with life."

"Okay."

I said "okay" because that is what the shrink and my grandmother wanted to hear. But I never stopped talking to my parents, just out loud. I found it was more acceptable this way. Through all of my tough decisions in life or times when I just missed them, I would hear my parents in my ear giving me encouragement. I would whisper back just so only they could hear. And so it was.

When I was nine, my grandmother took me to church. I think she wanted me to learn about where my parents were. She would always say something like, "I bet your mom and dad are up in heaven right now, playing backgammon with Jesus." I would giggle, not because her joke was funny, but because my mom was actually in the laundry room and my dad was raking leaves out back.

As I grew older, the images of my parents faded, but their voices were always clear. They told me to eat broccoli, play baseball, and everything else a parent advises their son. We even had fights. When I graduated high school, I wanted to move into the city where the people were young and fresh and the atmosphere was fast and exciting. If they had their way, I would never enter that city again. I turned their voices off for the first time during that argument and I left for the city the next day. We didn't talk as much after that. They would occasionally ask how I was doing or check to make sure I was eating right. Usually conversations were short and to the point. The incident on the subway was the first time I had talked to them in months and even then, they came off as unconcerned. So I joined the army.

I figured if they really didn't care about me, I would smite them the best way I knew how, enlist. Before my parents died, they had a talk with me at least once a week about the war. My dad would catch a snippet on the news about another bombing overseas and add a comment like, "More killing for nothing, Frank. That's all war is, just stupid killing." My mom would overhear us and yell into the parlor, "Frank, I don't want you ever joining the army, okay?" I would nod accordingly and continue my daydream.

After my grandparents died, I was just under 18, so Tom's parents agreed to take over custody until my birthday. I continued to live in my parent's house in my same room until college. I sold the house and bought an apartment on the east side. I was at a point in my life of daring and future. I put the past behind me the only ways I knew how, but it was no use. My parents were still there with me.

I entered the army with little clue and less intelligence about war. My parents had always shielded me from that. But as I quickly moved up ranks, I began to learn from the other soldiers and started to put pieces together of the events of the last decade and a half. I wrote an essay during one night in Rifle Company Thirteen. I was actually in a hospital bed with my left arm in a sling and no TV. It had been a rough night. So I wrote. I wanted to document everything I had learned up to that point in my military career in case God was wrong and something did happen to me in war. Here's my essay.

The United States was limping away from a tiring war in Iran. The people knew it had lasted too long, the media knew it lasted too long, and now the president knew it had lasted too long. American casualties were small compared to past wars, but many were still unsure of what had been accomplished. The liberal journalists made sure that live footage of villages being plundered and babies being killed were all that were shown. In one instance, a car bomb killed an American soldier in Shiraz and his 2 friends retaliated with a gruesome killing spree that rained blood over 25 innocent civilians.

U.S President Hallings declared a pull out of all troops on September 21st and the Army had finished its exodus back home by the next May. When Former President Starks entered Iraq, his goal was a democratic government and a steady set of representatives for the barren Middle Eastern country. Neither was accomplished. Instead of controllable leadership, there was only white noise blasting through the eyes of each member of the council. Two superior leaders were shot at point blank range during a session in the first month. There was never an acceptable candidate for president which led to cliques forming within the legislature; each believing their own disciple was the right man for the job. Months went by with no control and no progress.

In August the next year, the legislature fell apart. During a session between the diplomats and representatives from a large oil company on the border of Kuwait, words were passed and a lone gunman seized the life of men from both groups, 7 total, before committing suicide. This was the last time any trace of law was found in Iraq. 3 days later, the cliques that had been forming, staked their claim. They divided up certain parts of Iraq; mostly abandoned areas in the desert where their family names were rich. As for the areas that they did not agree on, they would handle this with blood.

Iran's President Mahmoud Ahvizor saw an opening for power in Iraq's discontinuity. Having already built a nuclear weaponry system greater than the United States, Ahvizor started looking for bargaining chips. He began, one by one, buying off pieces and parts of Iraq from different groups. He first would buy the businesses, then the community, and finally the land.

This practice was similar to that of 1900 mob bosses and therefore earned Ahvizor the nickname "The Iranian Godfather". Time magazine coined the term and put it on the cover of the July Issue. In that issue, references were made to Iraqi civilians who compared Ahvizor to "an international bully" and "Hitler reborn". It was clear to the United States that Ahvizor was building a more powerful and dangerous Iran, but it was not in the country's best interest to go to war on these simple presumptions.

In the next election, Jeffery Hallings became the new Republican president. Once again, the democrats had a split ticket and since Hallings promised a removal of troops from Iraq, he became a sure win for the Republican Party. As promised, Hallings had all U.S. Forces removed from Iraq by August of that same year, one month after the Time issue. Relations with Iran became sour when talks between the Hallings and Ahvizor started. Unlike Starks, Hallings was unwilling to compromise on some issues regarding nuclear power and undocumented weaponry. Several times in the early onset of war, Hallings requested that Ahvizor supply the

U.N. with a list of all military operations in Iran and its new Iraqi provinces. Several times, Ahvizor refused.

And so it began.

On February 13th, the following year a massive Iranian air strike lit up the streets of Washington D.C. at 2:40 am. It was later concluded that the strike consisted of 2 stealth F-18s dropping a combination of 4 missiles and unleashing 24 rounds of heavy fire onto the Washington Monument, the Congressional Archives building, and the west wing of the Department of Defense. Overall, only 340 people were killed, but centuries of documentation and security were obliterated within 8 minutes. The attack was extremely well planned and virtually undetectable, assumed to be performed by a high level member of the Iranian government. Immediately, Ahvizor was accused. He swore that he was not involved in any attack against the U.S. but evidence could prove otherwise. But, before any case had time to be built against Ahvizor, he was executed at his home in Bangladesh. A militant group formed from neo-Iraqi militia took it upon themselves to kill their self-proclaimed leader out of fear that the United States would retaliate and again cause innocent lives to be lost in the Middle East.

Hallings agreed that attacking the people of Iran would not solve the crisis at hand and did not show any threat to the Middle East or the premise of war. After Ahvizor's death, the case against him became less and less of a priority and eventually it was accepted that he was the sole conductor of the D.C. strike. When his colleagues and fellow leaders were interrogated, they either denied everything, or they admitted they had heard he was plotting something, but refused to get involved. It was a lose-lose situation.

When Ahvizor died, a diplomatic colleague of his, Khidir Hadi, replaced him as the new president of Iran. Unfortunately for Iran, Hadi was not near as strong a leader as Ahvizor and couldn't keep the country in check in these harsh times. Iran and Iraq again disbanded and engaged in a brutal civil war. The Iranian government in power, led by Hadi, claimed the rest of Iraq that was not yet theirs and formed the New Republic of Iran. But three-fourths of former Iraq and now half of Iran was run by Guerilla warfare groups or an anti-Iran militia who called themselves "Masha'allah" (Arabic for "God's will"). The Guerilla groups were reckless, lower-class infidels that used size and randomness to their advantage against Hadi's men. On the other hand, the Masha'allah had much control of the weaponry left over from the first Iraq war. Hadi knew he could not last much longer in his own country.

In August two years after the attacks, President Hallings and Iranian President Hadi co-signed a declaration of war against the Iranian terrorist organizations. Hallings was pushed into the war by an overwhelming support from the legislatures. Oil prices had sky rocketed to over 4 dollars a gallon in the US due to the complete shut down of all energy plants in Iran. Those plants that were not shut down were eventually taken over by the Masha'allah and forced to close. The Masha'allah understood that with enough political power and physical presence, they could reclaim the Iranian cities. Since oil was the only major player in this war, the UN and other council did not back the United States' decision and observed that this was a civil war, not a global problem.

US Troops were deployed in November and met with hostility. The first Iraqi war was slow moving and most of the killing was done from air or by snipers 200 yards away. The second war was much different. There was a 3-way battle between Guerilla militia, the Masha'allah, and US/Iran troops often resulting in hand to hand combat in which you would watch your enemy die in front of your eyes. The US plan of attack was to focus on the Masha'allah first, and deal with the Guerilla militia as needed since they were much less organized. Unfortunately, the US underestimated the Guerilla power and found they were often greatly outnumbered on the front lines.

Half way through the first year, the US/Iran troops were called to carry out a distinct extermination of all Masha'allah infidels codenamed Operation Desert Hunt. Although US/Iran troops conquered over half the major missile sites across the country, many still remained and budget and morale were low. The Guerilla militia could sense this and began their series of attacks. Through lack of organization, the Guerilla forces were obliterated except for a few remote areas in the rural regions. The Masha'allah grew in power at the few cities they still clung to, along with much of the Persian Gulf coastal region. Throughout the next few years, the war became much like North and South Korea. Whenever one force crossed into the other's territory there would be another opposite force to push them further back. And so it continued.

President Hallings had one more year in office and wanted to leave a strong Republican presence before leaving. It was concluded that the majority of the Iranian oil fields were again operational and what power the Masha'allah did have was not a threat to Americans, only their Iranian brothers. When US left the Middle East, they left a land of much war to come. Hadi was still the official Prime Minister of Iran and controlled roughly 80% of the land and resources, but the Masha'allah still controlled the coastal region and three or four major missile launch sites. Hadi desperately wanted to put an end to the Masha'allah rebellion. As long as they were alive, he was in danger. This is where his ties with American democracy came in his favor.

Back before the war, President Hallings and Prime Minister Hadi had a discussion focused around the idea of spying on the Masha'allah operations and taking out many of their major leaders in order to put an end to their rebellion. Hallings agreed under the condition that Hadi was to have no involvement in this plan and that any newly reclaimed oil fields would now be the property of American business. Hadi agreed and Hallings got to work. Along with only the Defense Secretary, Hallings created the most elite task force in the modern world consisting of a dozen of the best military officers that existed and creating an operation of Special Forces. This project was codenamed Blue Flag and became operational in the Fall before the war. Under the supervision of Hallings, 5 Special Forces agents killed 8 of the highest priority officers involved with Masha'allah. Up until the end of the war, Hallings continued to send in these men to accomplish tasks that otherwise would be considered a war crime under the revised UN regulations. Two months before the deployment date, 6 of the Special Forces agents exploded at a Masha'allah missile test site on the coast. Hallings covered up the men's identities and decided to dim the project.

Hallings kept tabs on the remaining men as well as begin to recruit others via the Patriot Act. Through phone taps and video monitoring, Hallings was able to keep close watch on the rest of his original 6 agents. He caught one of the men selling secrets to an Iranian official on business in Boston and Hallings ordered the traitor to be executed by another agent. When Hallings term ended, so did the task force, except for three highly skilled individuals he had trained at Gauntanamo. These three men came to be codenamed "Wise Men" and were a pivotal role in the destruction of the Masha'allah. They reported only to Hallings and were not to affiliate themselves with any US personnel. Hallings once described the Wise Men as "a simple solution to a terrible problem". In September, I was promoted to Rifle Company Thirteen. His simple solution became very, very complicated.

12

As to be expected, word quickly got back to the Colonel about my contest at the shooting range. He was even more impressed than he had already been. After a week of debriefing and learning the proper sniper tactical operation procedures, Goose and I became the First Team Snipers from Rifle Company Thirteen. We were the best duo the military had to offer and we could care less.

"Dude," Goose said during dinner one evening, "Do you think First Team Snipers get free access to the snack bar?"

"I doubt it, why?"

"No reason. I was just craving some Reese Pieces and I don't have any money on me."

"Yea. I doubt the snack lady would really care if you're a sniper. That is, if she *is* a lady. Have you seen that crust-stache she's got going?"

The colonel sat down. "Good afternoon men. A couple Majors and I will be discussing a new strategic opportunity in the Gulf this afternoon and I need both of you there for input."

"Hey Colonel," started Goose, "Do we get free access to the snack bar?"

"What? N-no. Why? Guys, stay on task here. The meeting is in the map room at 1400. Okay?"

"Yessir," I promptly said trying to make up for Goose's lack of interest.

"Sir, yessir!" shouted Goose. "And I'll bring a written request for sniper privilege in the snack bar." Colonel looked back with a non-humored glance. "Just kidding, sir."

In the map room, we shook hands with the Majors of two coastal divisions and made small talk until the meeting started. Major Davidson began. "Gentlemen, I've called all of you here because of a very rare and urgent opportunity in Ahvaz, Iran."

Goose and I perked up at this. We had been stationed in Saudi Arabia since the beginning of our enlistment and usually didn't hear much about Iran. In the states, Iran was always shown as a disbanded country in which the U.S. was no longer involved in. As far as either my or Goose's concern, Iran was a ticking time bomb. The Major continued.

"Ahvaz is a growing city near the border of Iraq and only a few hundred miles from this camp. We've been given permission from Iraqi personnel to cross through their country in order to get to Ahvaz. This took a lot of manipulating, but it is done and the opportunity now presents itself."

The suspense of this "opportunity" was killing me.

"At 1900 hours tomorrow evening. A four-man team of explosive experts and a two-man team of snipers will sneak into the city."

Colonel checked his stare in our direction.

"The mission for these soldiers will be simple. There is a spy working in Ahvaz who goes by the name of Thomas Baylor. He is an American who snuck through our system some years back and is now selling secrets to the Masha'allah terrorist group. We finally have conformation of his whereabouts and we are sure he will be leaving the Ahvaz Commerce Building tomorrow night."

The names and places that Major was throwing out were bouncing off me like rubber, but somehow Goose seemed deeply intelligent to the situation. I whispered to him, "Do you know what he's talking about?"

"Not a clue," he whispered back. So much for being intelligent.

The Major started with procedure. "At 1900 hours, we will have the explosives unit stationed at the south side of the Commerce Building. The unit will be ordered to place series of devices at the south and east entrances of the building. The sniper team will take loft on the roof of a nearby hotel we have bought out for the night. At

1915 hours, there will be a command on the radio to detonate the explosives. This will cause Baylor to exit the building through the North wing of the building, in range of the snipers. The second that Baylor's identity is confirmed and he steps in the streets, the sniper team will take him down. As the chaos is occurring, the Explosions Unit will be driving a non-military Jeep parked at the hotel around to the north side of the Commerce Building. Both teams will exit the scene via the Jeep with Baylor's body in tow."

Goose and I were dead quiet. Neither of us had had a real mission before. Not one that required any thought anyway. It had usually been the standard "shoot to kill" method. But now we had a plan, a task, and a timeframe. Not to mention the risks.

"There will be a series of risks involved in this mission. Baylor often does not travel alone and might even have body guards shielding him out of the building. The snipers will have to react to the moving target."

Goose leaned back in his chair with hands folded behind his head as if to say, "No sweat."

"All soldiers involved in this mission will be wearing street clothes and carrying no identification. If you are captured or killed, there will be no recognition by our government to the involvement of the bombing. We want the civilians who witness the event to see our soldiers as, for lack of a better word, terrorists."

He was right, there wasn't a better word. The meeting ended with handouts of gear and timesheets for the next day. The job seemed overwhelming, but Goose and I could sense adventure in each other as well. We

110

introduced ourselves to the Major after the meeting had finished.

"How old are you soldier?" he directed toward me.

"Twenty three sir."

He shook his head and sighed. "So is my son. And you can handle this job tomorrow?"

"Yessir. I'm the best shooter in the Army, sir, and I won't let you down." Best shooter in the Army had a nice ring to it.

"Then good luck to both of you." And he saluted his way out of the room.

The night went quickly with no sleep and no chatter. We ran through time schedules, tactics, and most importantly, Thomas Baylor's file. My first look at the man was on a black and white printout handed to me with a caption at the bottom, "Dangerous." I looked at the caption and back at the picture. Thomas Baylor looked to be older, have smooth, salt and pepper hair, and very charismatic, but "Dangerous" was not a word to describe him. He looked more like a friendly uncle than a double agent, but who was I to judge. He would be dead soon enough anyway. In the morning, we were in a humvee headed to Iran.

It was a long drive to the city. The roads were less like roads and more like packed earth. We occasionally came across a group of migrant workers or a small shanty town. Everyone in the town would stop and stare at our vehicles kicking dirt in the air as the tan humvees rolled past. I would often catch the face of a young girl or a teenage boy, but I couldn't tell if their frown of disdain was towards us or if they were looking for our help. It didn't matter anyway. We had other business at hand that affected much more of the Eastern world, not just this shanty town.

After eight hours of driving, the driver pulled to the side of a gas station outside the city. The gas station looked like an American gas station, but from the 1950's. There were classic signs for Coca Cola, and Pennzoil black and yellow was displayed on every window. "This is what it meant to be Americanized," I presumed. A stiff wind caught the side of my body and sent me ducking my face behind my hand. A girl came up to me with an umbrella. In broken English she said, "You like to buy wind protector?"

"Er, no thank you." I casually smiled and wondered to myself if she even knew the real purpose of the device. It looked like this area hadn't seen rain in years. We got back to the car and grabbed our gear. The driver told us this was the last stop he could make and we had to make the rest of the journey by foot.

Ahvaz was about 5 miles away. We made the walk quicker by telling jokes and the older men indulged us with stories of dirty women and younger days. We were all wearing business casual clothing and carried our artillery in large luggage. Lucky for our luggage, the road got gentler as we approached the inner streets of the city. At 1800 hours we were in the hotel checking out a deluxe upper level suite. We entered the hotel room and I immediately ran and jumped on the bed. The pillows had a certain peace that was long overdue. The Explosives Unit grabbed the keys to the Jeep lying on top of the

nightstand in the room and left into the night. Goose and
I stayed in the room a little longer assembling my gun
and holding on to the essence of civilian life. On any
other night, out of the Army, I would have considered this
to be an elegant suite with a beautiful view of an
otherwise meager town. Tonight, however, I hardly even
noticed the window.

After assembly and a quick run through of the
agenda, we were on the roof. Goose found a sharp nook
to hide behind and a perfect angle towards the front doors
of the Commerce Building. We sent out a radio message
to the commanders and the Explosives Unit stating our
position and situation. Time was all we had left to care
about.

After a call back from the commanders, the plan
unfolded. At 1915, a blast, and the Commerce building
was shaken. Goose watched through his binoculars and I
through my scope at the large pillars holding the
structure upright, then crumbling to the sandy streets.
As expected, a small number of people scurried out of the
north side of the building; one in particular was Thomas
Baylor. Goose spotted him first. "Baylor's out. Two
guards with him. Front and left. You've got a clean shot
between the two."

"Got 'em," I said. I took close aim and went
through the proper steps to assassination. "Can I
confirm positive target?"

"Target confirmed."

"Can I confirm motion to take a shot?"

"Motion confirmed," said Goose as he squinted hard
through the binoculars.

I took aim through the scope. Everything was green because of the night vision lens. I caught a glare off of a necklace on Baylor's chest. My crosshairs moved up to his head and I fired. Baylor dropped cold and dead onto the sidewalk. His guards immediately took notice of their boss's strike. They first looked at him, then to the rooftops, then back to him. It would have been impossible for them to see us. After a moment of Baylor being lifeless, they ran. Crowds were starting to form around the building, but we didn't stay long enough to notice. Goose and I hustled down a dozen or more flights of stairs and bolted through the back exit of the hotel. The Jeep squealed up seconds later. We jumped in the back and there was Thomas Baylor, still warm, but without air.

I was the closest to him. I emptied his pockets and everything I grabbed I would study and hand to the next person in the car to be radioed in. The Jeep swerved through the streets of the city like a formula one car banking every turn. I finally dug into Thomas' pocket and pulled out a hefty wallet. There, lying on top, was his driver's license. It was a Virginia license like mine but older, and faded. I verified the date of birth through the radio and continued onto the next card, a frequent shopper card from a Piggly Wiggly store from the states. I chuckled at the casualty of having this card and being a double agent, as if he was working for a competitive baker. I continued through the cards faster.

There were check cards, credit cards, visas, and then I finally landed on something too eerie and stopped. The card was getting heavier and heavier as I held it, and

I felt my eyes start to go black and my heart speed up. This card was another driver's license, also from Virginia. The name was Benny Angel.

I stared at the card in fear. Another soldier saw me start to shake and asked if I was okay. At this, the other soldiers and Goose turned to look at me. I took a deep breath and I said, "I knew this man. My dad worked with him."

Everybody was quiet until someone whispered, "what?" The soldier next to me looked at the dead man in the back and back to the picture he was holding. The government file on Baylor came up with a half dozen aliases, but none of them were Benny Angel. The soldier in charge of the radio insisted that we call this in and make sure everything was right. I immediately fought against it. There was something bigger happening here. The soldier deferred my request.

Just as the soldier put his finger on the radio, there was a loud *bang!* and the front of the car was ripped off. The remains of the vehicle tumbled forward and were sent spinning into a wicked roll. I don't remember much after that, except when I woke up. I opened my eyes to flames and metal. I was still strapped into my seat and Goose was next to me, slightly unhooked from his. I tapped him.

"Wh-wh."

"Goose, I think our car blew up." I looked around for any new information. There was a puddle of gasoline inching its way towards us. The two soldiers in the back with us were not moving. I assumed the two in the front of the car were killed by the blast. "Goose, we've got to get out of here. There's gasoline."

"O-Okay." Goose was a zombie, but an active one at that. My left arm was badly injured with blood running everywhere and my elbow felt certainly broken. I unhooked my seat belt with my right hand and slid at a downward angle off the seat. Goose was quick to follow. He was not as badly hurt, but was still dazed on the situation. I yelled at him to keep following me. We hobbled off the road and into a soft spot of sand and collapsed. I tried my radio. Only white noise.

Whoosh! The rest of the car exploded into a fireball from the gas leak. I covered Goose with my jacket since he still wasn't thinking about helping himself. In the distance I could here sirens still racing through the city. I knew that soon, they would be here. I got in Goose's face. His eyes were drooping, but I spoke slowly.

"Goose, we've got to get out of here, now. I need you to run with me for only a half mile or so." He nodded and stood under his own power. We took off in a lucid jog.

After 30 minutes or so, we fell in a heap behind a motel dumpster. There was a payphone there and I called back to camp. I don't remember much after that, but apparently they got the message. I passed out behind the dumpster with Goose against the wall. We were tarnished. I closed my eyes and went into a drunken state of war.

When I opened my eyes, everything was white. White sheets, white walls, white light. I was in a hospital bed in Saudi Arabia and Goose was shaking me.

"Frank. Wake up Frank. Frank."

"I'm up. I'm up."

"You alright bud?"

I felt like I had been in one of Sir's midnight fights. I was bruised down my sides and my left arm was in a sling. A feeling of aching was swimming through my body.

"Yea. I'm fine." Then I started to remember. "Goose, you didn't tell them anything yet, have you?"

"No, I just woke up a few minutes ago. I was just seeing if you were dead."

"Great. Thanks. Okay, do you remember about the guy we killed last night?"

"Yea. And how he was your dad's friend and all?"

"Exactly. We're going to need to keep that quiet for a little longer. Just until I sort this whole thing out."

Goose was sincere. "I understand Frank. I would be freaked out too if I just killed my dad's friend. No problem here."

"Thanks."

A few minutes later, a highly decorated man in a green uniform and thick mustache swept through the curtains. It was Major Davidson. He started.

"Hello, gentlemen. I'm sorry to say this is not the circumstances in which I wanted to see you again. But, life has a way of changing its course doesn't it?"

I couldn't tell if this was rhetorical or not. "Er, yessir," I seethed in pain.

"Ah ah. Save your strength Frank, I just need you to listen. It seems there is something peculiar about last

117

night besides your accident. The accident was tragic, yes, but the irony of the whole situation is even more exciting." The major was reciting to the walls and curtains with one arm behind his back like a Shakespeare performer. Also, he seemed to have no remorse for the rest of the soldiers that died in the explosion. He continued on point.

"You see Frank. The man you killed last night was a man you knew."

Goose and I exchanged looks of confusion.

"It seems you killed an old friend of your father's, a war buddy."

At this I had to interject. "With all do respect sir. I did see the man's driver's license last night before the explosion and recognized his name immediately. But my father, he was not in the military or the war for that matter. He must have known him in other circumstances."

"Ah. Then your father did keep his word." The Major thought hard on this. "Meet me in the dining room at 1200 hours. It seems there is much you don't know about your father."

A salute and he was gone amongst the sheets. I looked at Goose who was still confused.

13

Now, I'm writing from a hotel room in Venice, Italy. Don't ask. I just thought I should stop my story at this point and give you a disclaimer. Every thing that has happened in the book so far is true. I've had three dreams in my life, two have come true, and the final one tells me I'm going to save the world. My parents died when I was 8. My grandmother died at 14 and my grandfather at 17. I've only really loved one woman, and I lost her a long time ago. I joined the Army at 21 and became the best sharpshooter in the free world at 23. Like I said, everything that has happened to me is true. That is my irony.

I'm in Venice now. The only thing good about Italy I have yet to find, is the raisins I'm eating right now (I can't even make this stuff up). These raisins here are better than anything I've ever eaten in American snack mix or those crumbly little boxes. These raisins are full of quench and flavor. I can't imagine a snack like raisins changing that much over an ocean, so I have more of a belief that *I* am the one who has changed.

Before I joined the Army, I was typical. Dry routines through an active city. Dark corners of wild parties. I watched others live their own lives, but in doing so, I was neglecting mine. That is why I joined. I didn't know it at first, but that's what I believe now that I look back on it.

Ever since the day I shot Benny Angel, my life has been a photo book. Everyday, I wake up with a list of impossible tasks, and I get them done before lunch. Everyday, I walk through streets of foreign nations with bright lights and music pouring out apartment windows, and I hum to the music. The way I see it, Benny Angel wanted to die as much as I wanted to live. So that is what I'm trying to do. Live.

Major Davidson arrived promptly at noon. Goose, who had been released earlier that morning, was now grabbing a sandwich and sitting down next to Major. The nurse didn't think I was well enough to be moving around so I had her push me into the cafeteria in a wheel chair. I was a few minutes late and Major was waiting. He looked down at his watch that displayed 4 different time zones and then back at me.

"A little late, aren't we soldier?"

I wasn't quite how to respond to the remark. "S-sir. I'm still badly inju-".

"Never mind, we haven't got time to chit chat. I believe you are waiting for some explanations." He glanced around to see if anyone was eavesdropping and then softened his voice. Major was a gruff man. His face was smooth and sun burnt from 25 years in the desert and he always wore his cap to hide his less intimidating bald spot. His words were kind.

"Benny Angel was a very confused man. He became a rogue officer after two years in the service, but we caught him right away. He was tried and sent to Gauntanamo Bay prison for a life sentence although he never admitted to anything other than following orders from superior officers, but he never gave us names. And then it got interesting.

"After 4 years, we caught another rogue agent in the Gulf that we assumed was named Tyler Robinson, but was identified and pleaded guilty as Benny Angel. He looked nothing like the man we had arrested 4 years earlier, but his file and background information were synonymous to the first Benny."

Major was starting to get a little tense as he was talking and is voice rose a little after every pause. "We then went back to the first Benny and questioned him again. Still, he gave no names and pleaded innocence throughout various tortured methods. He was a rock and there exists no rocks in Gauntanamo. We let him go and arrested the new Benny, who we continued to call Tyler Robinson for the sake of our sanities. Tyler died in prison a year later. Meanwhile, Benny reported back to active duty and again worked his way up through the ranks until after another 3 years, he disappeared. Dropped off the face of the goddamn earth."

My head cocked. "What do you mean sir?"

"Well, one day he and a few soldiers were on a standard operation in Baghdad and then poof. The soldiers said they turned their head for a split second and he was gone. Probably ran off and met up with an old chum we presume. Of course, we didn't tell anyone that. We immediately reported that Benny was killed that day in Baghdad like many other soldiers and the secret was kept between his fellow comrades and me. Out of a streak of misfortune, the other soldiers were killed later that year in a car bombing and I quickly became the only one who knew about Benny Angel.

"Two years ago, I was touring Saudi Arabia just as we started to pull out of Iran. I was on the radio with a young soldier in combat. He was giving me information of a couple of our military officers that had been killed in a raid and was reading off their dog tags for me. The soldier read one as Benjamin Angel. I felt like I was going to have a stroke so I had the soldier bring in this man for me to look at. It wasn't the Benny I knew, but another soldier could identify him as the real Benny stating that he had spent 5 months in training with him and he never had used another name."

I noticed Goose had not touched his sandwich since Major had started talking.

"Like I said, this was interesting indeed. Well, two months ago, I got a tip from an old friend of mine in Ahvaz. He is a US diplomat who travels there often and said he was introduced to Benny at a gala one evening. The man called Benny introduced himself as an Iranian war profiteer who was in hiding from the Iranian government. My friend thought the name sounded familiar and thought he'd have me to check it out. That's where the stint started. The rest, you know.

"Benny Angel, the Benny *I* knew, was killed last night by you and your team. Ironically, we found that the bomb under the car was American made, most likely by Benny's men. You see, Benny Angel was indeed a man with two sides, neither of whom wanted him alive, and it seems he knew the jig was up and wanted the last laugh."

Major stopped his speech and smirked with confidence at Goose and I. My face was puckered and I was still rendering everything that was just said. It finally all sank in and I had questions. "Sir. If I may ask? How does Benny Angel relate to my father at all?"

"Well Frank. Right now, we don't believe he does. We've looked for everything and we know that your father was a perfect soldier and Benny was not, it just doesn't fit. We think the two might have just been friends through friends or something like that."

"Yes yes. About that. You said this morning that my father was in the Army. How come I never knew about it? And how long was he in the Army?"

"I'm not sure I'm the one to tell you about this Frank, but seeing no one else is alive from back then, I'm your man." He sighed and started again.

"Your father became a soldier much like you. He was drafted in the later months of Vietnam when he was already 21. Instead of quickly getting out when his tour was over like the rest of the nation, he took the decrease in troops as an opportunity to move up in rank. And he did. Very fast, in fact. After 5 years, he became a Major and even commanded me for the early part of my career. He had been dating your mother for quite a long time and they got married when they had you. Your dad was 35. Immediately, he dropped out of the Army and started his day job and normal life that you saw as you grew up.

"Of course your father still stayed in contact with other Army officials, but the calls became less business and more personal as the years went on. In fact, when your parents were killed, dozens of leaders came to their funeral. The Secretary of the State, World Diplomats, members of the Defense Board; even I attended."

I thought a moment. "But I was there and I don't remember any military or government persons?"

"Ah, that's because of your grandmother."

"Your grandmother?" Goose turned.

"One hell of a wicked witch, that woman. I've fought in some of the bloodiest battles of the last decade and still have nightmares about her yelling outside the funeral procession. She told all of the military dressed

124

men and women that it was your parents wish for no one with military gear to be at the funeral. I don't know if that was true or not, but she made her point and so we grieved for your father in slacks and t-shirts."

I giggled at my grandmother. It was just like her.

Major had to wipe the eerie smile off his face. "But, yes, Frank. Your father was an excellent soldier and a better leader. And what he gave up for his family was something I could never understand. He loved you and your mother and he would be very proud of you today."

"But what about Benny Angel?" I said still curious.

Major looked at his watched and started up from the table. "Thanks to you, yesterday Benny Angel became a ghost. Now if you excuse me, I have a meeting with the General to tell him of your successful mission. You need to rest and think a little about what I've told you today. If you have any more questions, give me a call." Major gave a truthful salute and clomped out of the cafeteria. I and Goose and a half bitten sandwich sat in amazement.

"Wow," started Goose, "My dad was just a cook in the Army." I laughed at his sarcasm.

"That's pretty cool though," I began, "you know, about that Benny guy and everything. Now we can tell our kids that we killed a real, full-blooded, double agent."

"*You* killed him remember, I just watched though my stupid binoculars."

"The way I see it, I couldn't have shot him without you there, so, nice kill partner."

"Thanks bud. One secret spy down, dozens to go."

We laughed and enjoyed what was left of our lunch time before the nurse came to take me away.

Just as the nurse started taking me up the ramp, a familiar *clumping* came barging around the corner. It was Major and he was in a full sprint towards me. In fact, I was afraid he wouldn't be able to stop with the extra belly he was carrying.

He started his sentence before he had even reached me. "Frank, Goose, I need you both in my office right now."

The nurse protested, but to much failure.

"Look woman, I need this soldier in my office pronto. So I don't care if you push him or I drag him by his IV bag, but it needs to happen now."

The nurse, in a fearful panic, boosted me forward down the hall following Major and Goose in a race of speed. I smiled as I watched the other doctors pass by and lower their glasses at an overweight commander huffing mightily forward and a soggy patient in tow. The race ended in Major's office and the nurse parked me next to his desk. The phone was off the hook. Major silently thanked the nurse and hinted for her to leave. He picked up the phone and said, "I've got them sir, I'm going to put you on speaker phone."

A voice came on slightly fuzzy and scratchy due to the distance between locations, but tone of the voice was cheerful.

"Hello men. This is Jeffery Hallings as in former president Jeffery Hallings."

Major smiled and winked at us and motioned for me to say something.

"Er, Mr. President, it's an honor, sir."

126

"The honor is all mine son. I heard you did some good for the country last night. And better yet, you did very good for me. I need to see you both at my home in Alabama tomorrow evening. I've faxed Major a document of things you need to know before you get here, so run through them with Major, and tomorrow we'll talk."

Major scooted us a large blanket of papers.

I filled the silence. "Sounds good, sir."

"Excellent. And Major, you are authorized to run through these papers too, but these are to be marked as absolutely confidential and need to be burned immediately when you are through with them. Is that clear?"

The Major was confused. "Yessir, but why do th-"

"Read through the papers and burn them. You will never again speak of these...General."

Major looked at the intercom on the phone. "G-General?"

"Yessir. You've deserved it."

"Wow, thank you sir. A General."

Major looked like a little boy going to Disneyland. I was still in awe of the political twist of the military. The Major, although a great guy and all, was about one turkey leg short of a combo meal. I prayed quickly that I would never be under his command again.

"Don't worry, you won't," said God from behind the coat rack in the corner.

"Good, thanks. You know you're getting quicker at answering."

"Yeah, it's the low-carb diet." God was a smartass.

127

The former president hung up the phone and we all flipped to the top page of the stack simultaneously. The packet was a detailed account of what has been happening in the military for the last decade and how it related to us. Hallings spoke of his creation of the internal spying team, but refused to name names or missions. At the end of his letter he wrote that he was impressed with our work last night and that he wanted us to work on a bigger project that he would brief us on when we arrived in Alabama.

Goose and I watched in wonder as Major took out a lighter and burned the remains of the fax in a steel trashcan. The sparks were full of promise. I didn't sleep much that night, despite the constant orders from the nurse, so I wrote. I wrote an essay on the summary of what I had read in the letter from the president. It wasn't perfect, but it got the point across. Tomorrow there would be more.

Our plane touched down in Birmingham National Airport in the hot afternoon. It felt good to have humidity again. The sand and sun had wilted my skin over the last few years and as I stepped off the plane, it felt like I was sinking into a bath.

The president's house was an hour drive into the country, past picket fences and desolate meadows. It became eerie when we hit a more narrow stretch of road that had a few dozen crosses within ten miles. Each cross had a name and a date to signify the loss of a loved one on this road. It reminded me of the pictures of Arlington cemetery. Names and dates.

After miles of empty driving, a palace. The car pulled into a gravel drive protected by gorgeous bronze gates. The drive was slow and lengthy, but it had a purpose, it was building suspense. At the end of the drive, there was the biggest house I had ever seen. The wood frame was coated peach and had a light plum shade dusting the corners and windows. The roof was like a pyramid that broke at the bottom and created two wings on the side of it. The front door itself was immaculate. Perfect cherry lines with a rustic door handle attached. It was the perfect image of Alabama. That was of course until I met former president Hallings.

Instead of a butler or guard answering the door, he did it himself. Southern hospitality I supposed. "Well, hello men. Welcome to Alabama." He gave a hearty salute and extended his hand. I was the first to accept and wasn't ready for his bear claw handshake. I felt my thumb crack and held back a shutter. The former president was a gentle man with a firm grip. He had blonde parted hair combed to the side and still looked like he could beat you in a footrace if only his body was willing. The khaki suit he was wearing accented his bright smile as he pushed us into his house.

"It's an honor to meet you, President Hallings."

"Please, call me Jeff. C'mon in guys. Make yourselves at home."

The president carried on being absolutely gentle for the good part of the afternoon. We ate a large lunch filled with tender pork and red beans. We were given a tour of the mansion and all of the accomplishments that helped create it. The former president was letting us know how much power he still had. Later that night, his southern draw disappeared and we found the dark side of the man from Alabama.

We met him in his study at 7:15 sharp. There was a map laid out on the desk and the president was studiously thumbing through a handwritten text. The text looked to be an old journal of his with brown leather hide encasing the scathed pages.

President Hallings spoke with a voice two octaves lower than we'd ever heard from his skinny frame. "Uh. Sit down boys." He stopped thumbing and found the page he wanted. It was a journal entry he had written 3 days ago. He read.

"Today I received word that an elite task force in Iran found and killed former Lieutenant Thomas Baylor. I was sent a photograph of the man and it is indeed Thomas. There is now only one left.

When I created the Three Wisemen after the war, their purpose was to eliminate political enemies that get in the way of a, I'm ashamed to say, profitable war. For the majority of their time under me, they did just that. Thomas was the first to challenge me. He started making ties with an arms dealer in the east while still under my watch, so I tried to assassinate him. The plan failed and he slipped off the map. A few months later, Tyler went rogue as well, most likely following Thomas. So began the ultimate set up.

I worked closely with Major Davidson to arrange this. Major was the commanding officer over Thomas when he disappeared and so I held him personally responsible, and better yet, Major still believed Thomas was Benny Angel. By threatening Major, I knew he would hire out the best men to track them both down on purpose or not.

The following year, Major's men captured Tyler by mistake and sent him back to Gauntanamo as Benny Angel. I met him there a month later and shot him myself, it was covered up as a prisoner coup. I continued to hint to Major that the Benny he had found was not the correct Benny and he continued to work. Then, last night I got the phone call. One part of me was relieved as I looked at the photograph, but the other part only grew more fearful. The truth was, the third Wiseman, is still alive."

President Hallings closed his tired journal and looked at both of us sadly. "The third man is Daniel Finch. He dropped off my radar only a few months ago. He was last seen in Paris of all places, but it's likely he's long gone now." President Hallings sighed and then looked towards us with apology. "I'm sure you both have a million questions."

I knew from Goose's face that we had the same question. "Sir, what are we doing here?"

The former president laughed. "With all of my story telling, I almost forgot. Huh. I've been going over your files ever since I learned about Thomas' death and I'm quite impressed. I made some phone calls and to verify and it seems I'm correct in saying you two are the best rifle team in the military right now. Am I correct?"

Goose and I nodded with a "that's what everyone keeps saying" kind of look.

"Well the situation is this...two of my ex-best agents are now dead and the third has gone AWOL. Here I am, with the two best shooters in the world, who know the whole story behind my program, and I'm ready to rebuild." At this the former president slammed the desk in enlightenment.

"Men, I would like to hire you to be my new secret agents."

Goose started smiling very wide and I could tell he was not smiling at the opportunity that just presented itself, but at the fact that president Hallings sounded very dorky when he said 'secret agents'. He was trapped in a James Bond thriller.

I broke the silence. "Sir, I think both of us are honored at this offer," Goose shook his head in agreement, "but, it's been a long few days and I think we need some time to sleep on it."

"You're absolutely right soldier. Good man. Your beds are upstairs and I'm sure you'll find everything you need. But I must warn you. Tomorrow I'm going to be on a flight to Paris either with two new agents or not. You have until then to decide."

"Yessir. Thank you again for the hospitality sir."

Goose and I shuffled to the oversized doors in the den to let ourselves out. As soon as the door opened, two identical, black Yorkshire Terriers yipped and began nipping at our toes. They were harmless, but gave us a shock nonetheless.

"Oh, forgive them," apologized the former president, "they don't get much company I'm afraid."

"Er, they're cute," I said without really examining their cuteness.

"Yep, they're my babies." The president pointed. "That one is Benny and the other is Angel."

Goose and I stopped petting and turned to see the president standing, cross-armed, with a devious grin and a snicker of laughter. "Good night gentlemen."

14

We took the job. It would have been stupid not to. Goose and I talked for a short time about it before the trip, but our decision kept coming came back to what kind of life we would return to if we didn't take the job.

"What, you want to go back to the stink," Goose was shouting, "the dry and the sand and the stupid jocks kicking your ass every night?"

"Come to think of it, no, that doesn't sound too appealing."

"Well then, it's settled."

"You got to admit though, this shit were getting into now, it's pretty deep."

Goose thought on it a minute and returned, "Well, I'd rather live my own life than watch some other half-wit soldiers run it for me."

There it was...the sucker punch. It got me every time. I smiled at Goose for winning his case. I was a secret agent.

The flight to Paris was mostly business. The former president cycled the paperwork around. We were each handed new forms of identification. We became Benny Angel. When we landed, we were taken to another gorgeous house owned by the former president, although this one was stucco, and on a cliff. The president wasted no time to see for himself what we were both capable of. He took us to his shooting range.

I shot first, again proving my supremacy. Then it was Goose's turn. I thought about it a minute and then it occurred to me, I had never seen Goose shoot a gun in my life. I wondered if he was rusty. I wondered if he was nervous. *Pop pop!*

"He'll do," said the president. Goose hit the bull's eye twice mimicking my shot almost perfectly. We retired to the study.

At nine o'clock or so, we got our first job.

Goose drove a new Jaguar through the dim city lights of Paris, while I sat in the passenger seat going over the instructions again. It was a routine mission; kidnap one of Daniel Finch's closest arms dealers and bring him back to the president's mansion for questioning. Simple. Still, I was nervous.

The cobblestone streets didn't help my nerves as we bumped along winding in and out of tight corners.

"This thing handles like a dream," Goose shouted over the wind whipping through the open windows. I looked at him with a nauseous face and he politely rolled the windows back up. We rolled into a small villa at midnight and noticed a cluttered garage with a fluorescent light still burning. We spotted our target immediately.

The man we were hunting was a lanky one at that. He barely needed the extra length of the crowbar he held under the car he was working on, but he used it anyway. We approached quietly at first, and as we got closer, shuffled our feet to give hint of our presence. The lanky man slid from under the car.

"Good evening, gentlemen, is there something I can help you with?"

"Actually there is." Goose and I drew our 22mm pistols in unison. It was splendid.

The man looked only slightly fazed by the guns as if he was expecting us. All of a sudden we heard a barrage of boots clomping up behind us. It turns out he *was* expecting us. Goose and I raised our guns in the air and fell to our knees. Goose whispered, "Being a secret agent sucks."

We were herded inside the gorgeous establishment by two large, smelly men. We took a seat on a plush leather sofa and stared aimlessly at expensive art tacked to the Calcutta walls. The lanky man came in after working on his car and sat down across from us. He was calm and defiant. He, of course, wanted to know what we were doing at his house and quickly assumed we wanted to steal something. He just hadn't figured out it was him yet.

Goose and I remained confident for two reasons. One - because this guy was truly an amateur in home security and two - we had an extra set of handguns tucked behind our coats that the guards didn't bother to check. After the lanky man was done explaining the various torturing methods he has performed on common house thieves, I began my plan. I felt like I was on the subway again. I took control of the situation. Goose picked up on it right away.

"That painting over there...that's a nice *one*."

"Why yes, it certainly is. Is that the one you were planning to steal?"

"I don't know, that one is nice, *two*."

"Yes, they are both nice."

"But my favorite by far is the one with the *three!*..."

The cue. Goose drew quickly and shot the guard in the corner. I ducked and put a bullet in the guard directly behind us before he even caught his breath. We both went on the assumption that the lanky man did not carry a gun, and luckily we were right. Like I said...easy.

We got back to the president's home with the lanky man tied up in the trunk and two mischievous smiles on the faces of Goose and me. The president insisted that he would do all the questioning, so we were left to wander about the gorgeous house. My favorite painting was a depiction of Don Quixote riding alongside Poncho with windmills in the background. At around 2 am, the president called for us.

"Thank you both. And congratulations on your first successful mission." High-fives came next. "There is good news and bad news tonight. Good news is - this man gave us a good lead on Finch. Bad news is - I will not be involved in any part of the rest of your time here, or on any mission for that matter. You already know I have a family and my time with you hunting a ghost is not time well spent with them. Your next mission is here." He handed me a dense package. "I'm sure you are still very confused about everything that has happened in the last few days, so I tried to explain the rest in it. What is not explained, you will have to find out on your own. Good luck to both of you gentlemen. Oh, and you must remember, don't get caught, because if you do...". The president made a motion to lock his mouth. He gave an awkward salute as he walked out the door.

The next morning, we examined the package. It was pretty useless actually. There were lots of documents creating a timeline of Daniel Finch, but no patterns or methodology behind any of it. The president was right, Daniel Finch was a ghost. And as of last night, he was a ghost living in Rome, Italy. So we followed our ghost.

Paris was an elegant city, but Rome was history. Textbooks overflowed with the power and love and killing that had seen the streets of Rome. I strolled the same streets wondering if I would be the next chapter in those textbooks. Every waking minute I spent thinking to myself, I became more self conscious. I felt that I had gotten very lucky so far and my luck was sure to run out soon. I felt very scared. Then I remembered my dream.

The words scrolled through my mind, haunting me, teasing me. *Go ahead Frank, you're about to save the world.* I came out of my daydream when Goose shook me. We were in a hotel and the bell man wanted my bags. Goose was looking at me in an unsettling way.

"You okay man," he said, "you don't look that great."

"I'm fine. It's the damn jetlag."

With no former training in secret agent-ing, Goose and I started from scratch with a notebook and a lot of ideas. We began a stakeout. For the next few weeks, we enjoyed long hours at local hotels, casinos, and nightclubs looking for a dark haired, Spanish playboy we knew as Daniel Finch. The days were exhausting. We drained all of our energy staring through magnified lenses, squinting through strobe lights at the disco. It was endless. Finally, day thirteen, we found him.

We were walking up to a hotel called Casa del Rio. A long limousine was parked outside like many of the ritzy establishments in the area, but this one had an American embassy logo on the back. To our knowledge, no US Diplomat was due to arrive in Rome for another week at least, so we watched. Just then, like Jesus parting water, our man appeared. The golden doors of the hotel flew open and he came strutting out in Armani from head to toe, two exotic companions in his arms. He helped them into the oversized Lincoln and they took off for bigger parties. Goose took over from here.

"Ahem," Goose offered the desk clerk. He was using a phony, snobbish accent that was perfect for the situation. "The man that just left here, he dropped these as he was leaving." He put a pair of his own gloves on the counter.

"Who? Mr. Angel?" said a short, feminine voice behind the desk.

"Ah yes, that's the one. Benny I believe is his name. I met him last night at the casino and we lost track after that. Could I have his room number so I can drop his gloves off later this evening?"

"Well sir, Mr. Angel requested that his room number be kept private. I'm sorry."

"Mm hmmm," Goose continued in the annoying voice. "Well, if you see him, tell him that thanks to the lack of service at this hotel, his Four-hundred dollar gloves are in the loving care of a hobo on the street!" Goose left the desk, gloves in hand. The girl ran after him.

"Sir, sir! I apologize. Here, here's his room number." She wrote the number on Goose's hand as to not say it out loud. She scribbled 413.

"Ah, thank you my dear. You've been most helpful." Goose felt in his coat pockets for a large tip. When he couldn't find anything, he whispered to me in his normal American slang. *"Dude, do you have any money?"*

I whispered back, *"Dude, no."*

Goose stood back up to full grandeur and said, "I'm sorry my dear, but I have left my wallet in my room. I will surely not forget your kindness and I will tip you with the utmost interest the next time I see you." A little over the top.

"Whatever," said the girl.

As we snuck back to our own hotel, we were giddy. Now all we needed was a plan. After a few hours we settled on one, although quite risky, that seemed to work. The image of the president locking his mouth kept running through my head. This was not the Army anymore. If we failed, there would be no second battalion to back us up. We were very much alone.

The plan unfolded. For a week or so, we would stalk Finch's schedule, make notes of his habits, and find a time that became a pattern for Finch. This was harder than expected. The rogue turned out to be a random piece of dust flying around Rome. He never would leave his room for more than a few hours at a time, but never seemed to be alone either. He was protecting himself. We finally found a consistency. At 8:00 pm on Friday, Finch would be dining with an Italian diplomat. I overheard his advisor telling the desk clerk one morning when I was pretending to be delivering laundry.

The next step for our plan was a method of killing. No one could witness Finch's death, nor could any clues be left to an outside party involvement. If any hint of conspiracy were to reach his arms dealers, they would vanish and take their business elsewhere.

At 8:00, the plan became reality. As Finch was leaving the hotel, I casually waltzed into the grand ballroom and took the elevator to the 4th floor. I found the suite at the end of hallway. Using the copy of Finch's key, I turned the lock over and crept into the silent room, gun drawn. I flicked on the lights and started sifting through the rooms looking for cameras or other security devices. The suite was empty.

I slid under the bed, looking up at an expensive mattress. I took out a knife from my belt loop and slit a line down the length of it. I removed the majority of the spongy material so I could fit comfortably inside of it. I sent the rest of the material to a trash bag and then out the window to a loitering Goose four stories below. He came on the radio. "Are you ready?"

"Yea. I've got the mattress ready. Now we just wait." We knew it would be a while until our man returned so I took out my notebook and wrote to pass the time. Three hours later, Goose came back onto the radio.

"Frank, our man just pulled up. He'll be upstairs in about four minutes and he's got a girl and two guards with him."

"Perfect. I'm turning you off now."

"Okay. Good luck bud." Goose's voice was cut. I abandoned my position of writing on the floor and tucked my notebook into my pants. My body conformed to the awkward angle in the mattress. I took a deep breath and waited.

I heard a buzzing of drunken stupor coming down the hall. One of the guards fumbled for the keys and turned the lock. *Click.* A light jumped on and the guards entered, leaving Finch and the girl in the hallway falling all over themselves in drink and lust. The guards began their search. They checked everything from the curtains, to the cabinets, to under the bed. Nothing. My heart was about to implode in my rib cage. I could feel sweat building up on my forehead and it made me feel heavy.

The guards gave Finch the go-ahead and the drunken man thanked them both sincerely. He stumbled to the bed and him and the girl fell onto it in a fit of giggles.

The girl told him she was going to take a shower and instructed him to stay put. He obeyed. I could hear the girl give a wet smack on his lips and tiptoe off into the bathroom. When the shower turned on, Finch leaned up in bed to turn on the TV. I made my move. Ever so gently, I dropped out of the mattress and braced myself on the carpet floor. When I eased up into the freshness of the room, Finch was on the bed with his back turned to me. I quietly raised my silenced revolver and took aim at the back of his head. *Phap!* Finch's body doubled over with heaviness and rolled onto the floor. I stammered back into the mattress and tucked the gun back into my pants. I waited.

The shower was turned off and the girl could be heard blow drying her hair. She finally stepped into the room and dropped whatever she had been holding. It sounded like a wine glass when it splintered onto the tile in the bathroom. Instead of checking on Finch, she saw the blood and immediately ran towards the door. She was obviously not in love with the dead man. The door opened and she started bawling and screaming to the guards. They rushed in to see Finch's body, tarnished and blue. They gasped. They quickly started checking the windows the curtains, and then they saw the girl. They dragged her to the bathroom where they saw an open window and four storied below, a shattered hand gun. She pleaded with them. She was crying. The guard took out a gun and ended her life. He wiped the gun, put it into her hand, and both guards left the room in a frantic state.

I witnessed the whole scene from the tight spot in the mattress, listening hard for every detail. I felt badly about the girl, but she was just as wretched as Finch himself. We identified her the night before as a twice convicted serial killer who had paid off a judge in Belize. She was just as hopeless as Finch.

After the guards had clamored down the hall and out of sound, I left my nook and strolled out of the room. I met Goose at a bar on Main Street. When I walked in, he looked up from a mug and grinned in relief.

The bar was noisy and wet. There were larger women spilling beer on themselves much to the joy of skinnier men. The radio in the corner would play a few newer pop songs from around Europe and then switch to an older classic. Everyone knew the classics, except for Goose and I. They were sung in Italian.

As the song got faster, more beer was sloshed and more tenants dropped to the floor in numbness. The air in the bar was warm and sticking to my clothes. Shouts from every direction slingshot themselves through the fog and bounced back like a boomerang. A fat man with a large belly sat down next to us and looked into his mug like a sieve. He was looking for a future or a woman or an answer. He found neither and gulped down the drink in self pity.

Over the laughter lingering around the bar, Goose and I sat still and nervous. In the back of the establishment, we were letting the excitement of the night ease into a gentle slumber. We toasted to a successful mission, we toasted to a new lifestyle, and we toasted to a world without Daniel Finch. The beer turned into water after six drinks and we were wobbling to the exit of the bar. As we walked out, all around us were slovenly men and women with loose clothing and cheerful eyes.

At the exit, we stopped. There was a man in the door way in a navy blue pea coat, a white dress shirt and a white tie. The glow from the lamp post outside was bouncing off of his jet black hair and dancing onto the wine glasses beside us. He tucked away a wallet he was presenting to the bouncer and on the back of it was a patch of a skull sewn into the leather. Goose had noticed that I had stopped and did the same when he too spotted the figure. The man walked out of the light and into the bar with fierce eyes and a pointed purpose. I couldn't tell if he was an angel or demon, but neither would have surprised me.

He glanced around the soaked bar and without looking at Goose or I as he walked towards us. He approached the bar to the side of me and spoke forward.

"So, it is done, isn't it?"

There was no one in front of him to speak to. I looked around and didn't see any other reactions but my own. "Pardon?"

He turned to me this time. His eyes were deep coals. "I said your mission; it is done, isn't it?"

Goose turned whiter than his already pasty complexion.

I started again. "Do we know you?"

The man nodded to a bartender that walked by and stared back to us. "No, not yet." He slid a business card under his arm into our viewing range. "My name is Mateo. The president hired me to make sure you didn't screw up. And seeing that you didn't, it looks like the three of us are going to be seeing a lot more of each other now."

"The three of us?" Goose questioned. We looked down at the card. Mateo Jimenez. First Class US Navy Sharpshooter. And so we were three.

15

My skull hurts and my spine is piercing with agony on every move. My nose is filled with dry blood and my jaw hurts when I move to speak. I look around and there are four sterile, concrete walls with a barred doorway. The bars are old and rusted, but I can sense their strength. The floor is like the walls, cold, dusty. I am in a prison near Karkük, Iran.

I have been here for a few days now and I'm not sure about anything. The guards will not speak to me; they only shove a plate of hot food under the slit in the door. The men in suits do not torture me; they only ask how I am doing every few hours, then ignore me when I say "not good". This place does not scare me; it only lets my imagination run wild like a beast throughout this cell. So I've fallen back to writing. My writing has become harsher and more gothic. This is the first time I have been alone since college and it makes me nervous. My mind runs a movie reel over my life before war and I shutter at the images on the screen.

I start with my parents. They were so young to die. I was not ready to be on my own. My grandparents. Losing their son before they died themselves. I never talked to them about it, but I could sense their misery by the way they transported their bodies through the rooms of my house, like ghosts. My dreams. They were uncanny and brought nothing but pain to my life. They were good at first, but what joy they gave me diminished over time and left me with false hopes. I was meant to save the world at one point in my life. Now here I am, in an international prison, my friends are dead, and I am cold. I could care less about the world. My teeth start to chatter and the guard tosses a blanket through the rusty bars. His kindness is unnerving.

My mind keeps reeling and then freezes into slow motion on a girl with dark hair. It's Angela. She is on the screen in a flowing teal dress that she wore to church on Easter

Sunday. She is sipping lemonade on Fourth
of July. She is kissing me under the stars.
And now she is crying. My mind traces my
life like a fine pencil on a drafting table. My
life is complicated.

I had been in college for a year and not a single day
passed that I didn't thank God for my life. There was
always fun to be had. I had Angela and I was the luckiest
man alive. I went to bed early hoping for my first decent
rest of the week. The phone woke me up at 12:30 am.

"H-hello," I said groggily.

Angela was on the other end, crying, she couldn't
put together a sentence. I was scared. We met in the
park located halfway between our dormitories. It was
where we had spent many long beautiful nights.

On the walk over, the wind stung my face. My neck
huddled itself behind the collar on my denim jacket and I
shuffled along with my arms squeezed tight to my sides.
As I walked through a parking lot with my head looking
purposefully at the ground in front of my feet, a blinking
appeared in the corner of my eye. I looked up to find
nothing.

Again my head fell limp towards the pavement and
then another blink. This time I caught it. It was the
street lamp over my head. As I kept walking, each street
lamp would flicker as I walked under it.

Finally I came to a lamp that had a broken bulb
and was dark for the night. I stopped for a moment and
look at the light. *Blink.* It felt like it was talking a picture

of me. My breathing stopped and I picked up pace. The faster I walked, the brighter the lights flickered. I didn't want to admit it, but inside, I knew God was following me that night. I ruffled the collar on my jacket and returned to a brisk pace.

I saw Angela first coming out of the shadows next to a line of cold Elm trees. She had her hood tucked over her head and she meandered slowly through the wet grass. She never looked up, but she could sense me, and she extended her arms. We embraced and stood for a few minutes without a word. Finally, I got the nerve.

"What's wrong?"

She could barely hold herself with the weight of sadness on her shoulders. Again she said nothing and again I asked. Through a face of snot and tears she sobbed, "I'm late."

Even now, after having been shot at and tortured in the Army, I cannot remember a time when my heart stopped as forcefully as it did that night. I couldn't feel anything. My eyes went dry and my legs went weak. I fell under my own weight and pulled her to the ground in a mess. She cried louder and harder, but I could not cry at all. I was too busy thinking. *I was too young to be a father. We were just kids. Angela didn't deserve this.* My chest stayed heavy for the entire night and we did not sleep. We just lay in a pile of tears and sweat and spit and Angela prayed. I got into a position to pray, but didn't carry through. I just sat there, on the edge of the bed, hands folded gently, like a puppet. I felt ashamed. Reverend Dan's death was still too fresh in my mind. I hadn't talked to God in a couple of years and I didn't want our first conversation to be about this. I was too proud. So I sat and stared at the wall, or at my hands, or at Angela. I think she was praying for me.

The next day we went to the drugstore before the sun came up. The morning was overcast and full of illness. I felt that every living thing I saw was not worthy of gladness until they had faced the pain that I had. We went back home and Angela took her test. We waited. It was awkward. We couldn't talk about sports, or the weather, or TV. We just waited.

At 7:34 am the test was done. Angela was not pregnant. I let out a sigh of relief and I noticed my hands were shaking horribly. I grew up a lot that morning.

Angela and I broke up two months later. So it goes.

When Goose, Mateo, and I left Italy, I thought about Angela briefly. I saw a younger girl staring at me from across the street the morning we left. She had brown hair like Angela's, but that was where the physical similarities stopped. The thing that made me stop was that she was eating a raspberry gelato, Angela's favorite. Our taxi pulled up and she was out of mind again.

The three of us left Italy that night for the Middle East for two reasons. First, a long plane flight was the perfect time to get to know our new companion and secondly, we had another mission. With Daniel Finch out of the picture, it seemed the former president didn't want to waste anytime where the original Three Wisemen left off.

On the trip over the ocean we got to know Mateo. He was much less personable and much stricter than either Goose or I, which is probably why the president assigned him to us. After 10 hours, the only thing gained from the conversation was that Mateo was the highest level soldier possible. He ran through his resume a dozen times at least. Naval Academy - First in Class. Olympic Sharpshooter – Gold Medal. Navy Seals – Captain of First Battalion. I was impressed. He seemed to make it very clear on the flight that the business of war was the only business he would be speaking about for the next few months.

When we landed in Baghdad, we were headed into a whirlwind of political risks. So we wore costumes. We posed as journalists for the Washington Post. In the president's message he sent a list of targets and tasks for the next few weeks in Baghdad. He listed a dozen different Iraqi outsourcers. Some of them, I had heard their names mentioned on the news before, others were from Finch's file, but it didn't matter anymore. As our plane landed, the pilot had to do a quick loop and dive toward the runway as to avoid anti-aircraft missiles in the neighboring areas. The plane darted down with amazing speed and power then caught the wind with a heavy whiplash and ripped us down to earth. I threw up and Mateo looked at me with a face that said, *"What a wimp."*

I staggered off the plane and started clicking away on my camera to show the Iraqi civilians I was a photographer from America. They liked that. Young men posed with AK-47s and women shielded their faces from the lens. We entered the heart of the city via taxi and ended at a hotel on the major drag.

We spent the night with strategy and tactics. Mateo, despite his personal shyness, had no trouble sorting out elaborate plans and devising intricate maps and timelines. He was superb at this. Around 9:00 am the next morning, Goose and I rose to Mateo's alarm screaming at us. He was already up and had finalized the first mission by the time I hit the off switch on the alarm. That day, we began the most devious part of my life. For the next year, I was only Benny Angel.

The year went exceedingly fast and the three of us were flawless. Thanks to Mateo's perfect procedure, Goose's perfect eyes, and my perfect shot, we took down the most feared politicians and criminals in the world. True, most of our prey were not the most difficult to kill (they were mostly fat men who often walked the streets in broad daylight with only one or two bodyguards), but a job was a job and we did it well.

The former president would contact us every few weeks to check our progress and he was always pleased. So were we. After reading the files on our victims, and studying their filthy habits, we felt completely justified in killing every last one of them. They were concubines for money and power and did nothing but kill and rape and destroy what was left of freedom.

After I assassinated the final target with a 22mm bullet through the left earlobe, we took a few nights off. After seeing 28 men die through my scope in a relatively short period of time, I was exhausted. I retired to the hotel room on an ordinary Friday night and sat down with the first set of documents president Hallings had ever sent us, the ones Major Davidson had seen.

Most of the documents I had only skimmed over the first time and wanted to review them again now that I had matched names with faces in this part of the world. I stopped when I got to a page about Tyler Robinson, the first Benny Angel to go AWOL.

On the 18th page of the document, there was a written letter from Tyler to the former president discussing the possibility that a certain arms dealer in Iran did not need to be killed. He said after following the man for a week, it seemed the man was dealing completely with the US and his file should be reevaluated. The man was the Prime Minister of the Iranian Republic, Khidir Hadi. The letter was dated two days before Tyler was killed. It was postmarked in Iran.

I jolted back in my chair and read the last few lines of the letter again. It didn't add up. I skipped to a previous page in the document that stated Tyler was killed after being in Gauntanamo for a month. I kept reading. Further along in the documents was Tyler's death warrant from prison. It was verified by President Hallings.

I was alone in the hotel room that night. Mateo and Goose had gone to a local bar and were not around to answer my new questions. I called the president directly. There was no answer so I left a message. My message felt ill when I said it

"Er, hello President Hallings. This is Frank. Um. I was curious about a couple things and needed them to be cleared up. Give me call back." I hung up with no more knowledge than before. After another glass of bourbon and some more thinking, I wrote the president an email. About an hour later, an fax came to the room. It was a letter from President Hallings. The letter read:

Frank,

Thank you for your concern about Tyler's death. I'm sure it looks very confusing on paper, but I can assure you that he died a very legitimate death in Gauntanamo at my supervision. Tyler Robinson was an agent who tried to cover up his lies with an ignorant paper trail and it seems he succeeded in fooling you. I will be glad to talk to you personally about this when I see you next week in Baghdad. Until then I have another mission for you.

This mission is your most important yet and needs to be handled with great professionalism. We've been watching Iran's Prime Minister Khidir Hadi for the last few months. As you may know, Hadi is one of the United States' greatest war partners and ties with him have been fruitful for our country. Unfortunately, Hadi has recently acquired ties with the Masha'allah, the rebellious group in Iran. These ties could destroy any chance that the US has of winning this war. I need you to assassinate Khidir Hadi by this time next Thursday.

This mission is detrimental to our country's health and a generous future will be in store for you afterwards. When I see you next weekend, I will reveal all questions you have about Tyler Robinson and Khidir Hadi. Until then, good luck.

Sincerely, Jeffery Hallings

The letter felt sick in my hands. Before I could think anymore to myself, Goose and Mateo stumbled through the door reeking of Rum and cranberry.

"Frankie!" slurred Goose, "what's happening?"

Mateo was a little more conscious. "What's this? Another mission?"

"Yea. Hallings just faxed it over." Mateo skimmed the letter. He was confused on the part about Tyler so I tried to quickly explain. He shrugged it off and continued to the bottom.

"He wants us to kill Khidir Hadi!?" Mateo shouted.

Goose became much more sober at this. "What? The Iranian Prime Minister?"

"Yea."

Goose was dumbstruck. "Wow, we're really good. You know that Frank?" He was drunk again. "You and me, we're like superheroes or something, you know?" Mateo stared at Goose. "Oh, and Mateo too of course. Yea, we're like superheroes."

Mateo was showing signs of stupor himself and squinted at the shirt I was wearing. It was an old high school baseball shirt that said Rockets in bold blue letters across the front. "Yea, and you can be Captain Rocket," he laughed as if he had just said the most creative thing in the free world.

As I gathered a strong waif of Mateo's attire I coughed back. "You guys smell like cranberries!"

"And rum," countered Mateo in another fit of genius.

Goose smiled blissfully. "Yea, that's who we are. Captain Rocket and the Cranberry Kids." All of us broke into a symphony of uncontrollable laughter. And so I became a superhero.

16

On the corner of a windswept street in Karkük, Iran, I released the safety lock on my 22 millimeter handgun. I glanced at my watch and it read 5:58 pm Karkük time. Behind my dark Oakley's were two watchful eyes that were quickly and carefully rendering everything in their sight. A voice in my earpiece said, "He's a little late, more like three minutes now". I acknowledged this warning and wiped a handful of sweat off of my forehead. A group of noisy school children walked by with an older teacher. I couldn't understand a word they were saying and ignored them like a dull radio frequency.

I was an undercover Special Forces agent and I was minutes away from performing the execution of Khidir Hadi, the Prime Minister of the New Republic of Iran. The department of military intelligence in which I worked was non-existent. The only four people in government that acknowledged it were the President, me, and my two partners on this expedition. These two were Leonard "Goose" Banks and Mateo Jimenez.

Goose had staked out a spot on top of a warehouse on the middle of a road named Al-Qatar with a M40 Sniper Rifle and a bag of sunflower seeds. Mateo was in a produce truck around the corner running a satellite feed through his laptop keeping tabs on Hadi. He relayed the message that Hadi was approaching and I began a quiet pace down Al-Qatar. Into his headset, Goose went over the schedule one more time.

"Okay. Hadi is being driven here in the back of a black Escalade. The vehicle will back into the gates at 421 Al-Qatar, which is diagonal to my roof position. The guards will step out first. There are two of them, one in the left side door and one in the passenger seat. Since only Hadi knows the code for the building he will be escorted..."

Mateo interrupted Goose. "1 minute".

"...out of the trunk by the guards. When the trunk is opened, I take the first shot at guard number one. Frank will be within 10 yards of the vehicle and take out the second guard. You will then shoot Hadi from point blank range in the back of the Escalade. If the driver gets out, I will handle him. Frank will then disappear down Hasin-Quaida Way and we will all regroup at Hanger 14 at the Karkük air strip at 1900 hours."

Through my Oakley's, I saw the dark Escalade drag around the corner kicking dust into the eyes of the city. I took a deep breath and moved my fingers across my four day beard. I stopped behind a bread vendor and peered past the cart to the Escalade that was now 20 yards away.

Mateo came on the radio. "Target approaching. Goose, look for snipers in the windows and roofs."

"No one out here but me, amigo," said Goose.

The Escalade pulled past the gates and started backing up. "Alright, cover me Goose." I peeled around the bread cart and paced twice toward the vehicle. A well dressed, but dirty, Iraqi suit reared out of the passenger door and began to open the trunk. I lifted my weapon and took aim at the man. I heard the voice of Sergeant, yelling in my head.

"Look down the barrel like it's a woman, Frank, not some plaything! Be respectful, but confident. Be gentle on the trigger or you'll shoot high. Fire that sunofabitch, Frank! Two eyes, Frank! Two eyes!"

The latch on the trunk clicked out of place by the Suit and the door started to rise. Almost shyly, the man was struck twice in the back by my silenced gun. As the man dropped to his knees I took off in a dead sprint. Before the other Suit had any idea what happened...*phap phap phap*...three shots from Goose put him right away. My earpiece was giving me the go ahead. I reached the back of the Escalade and my heart dropped into my stomach. I was looking down my barrel at an already dead Hadi, whose corpse was duct taped to the back seat and was strapped with wires growing over his body like vines. Beneath Hadi's right elbow was a small illuminated box with stopwatch numbers counting down from 00:06.

I gripped reality and ran towards the street screaming "It's a setup, it's a mothafuckin' bomb!"

From two blocks away Mateo held his headset tighter to understand. He managed to get out a "wha..." just before he was cut short by a bone curdling blast. His headset ran into a high frequency pitch and stung his ears. He threw them down and took off running toward Al-Qatar. Five strides out of the truck, Mateo was tripped up by two bullets simultaneously slicing his calves. He lied in the street with blood running down his face from the fall. Two men with dark gold necklaces stepped up to Mateo's body, looked deep into his eyes, and pulled a life sucking trigger into his throat. Within minutes, Mateo had bled to death while the two men stood over him, waiting.

Goose witnessed the explosion through his scope. He immediately dropped his rifle and looked down towards me. All he could think is *shit,* but all he can scream was "Frank, get up Frank!" The rooftop had been his home for the last two hours. It felt good, it felt right, and now it would be his grave. A Suit with an AK-47 fanned him three times from behind a roof crest. Goose struggled to crawl to the edge of the roof and peered down at me lying motionless in the street. Veins rose to the surface of his face and his breathing was too quick to control. One final sweep from the AK-47 and Goose was dead.

All the people that once lined the streets with gifts and foods had now run to safety. The blast sent the Escalade rocketing 5 feet in the air and then landed on its side, spraying glass into the sandy road. I was laying face first in the hot dust with my legs sprawled and my arms soft to my side. A warm wind caught my face and my eyes blinked open. Being a trained killer, I had no time to recuperate. Keeping my form, I started analyzing my situation. My head hurt from the blow to the pavement that knocked me unconscious. I studied the dust from the blast still lingering in the air and figured that I was only out for a couple of minutes. *Whoever did this had ample opportunity to kill me after the blast.*

I climbed to my feet and rubbed the dust from his eyes. *Mateo and Goose!* I didn't remember anything after the explosion and look up to Goose's post. There from the edge of the ornate rooftops hung Goose's head and left arms drenched in crimson. I could already guess Mateo's fate. I spotted my handgun back near the Escalade and shuffled towards it. From around the corner came two black sedans with Iranian nationalists hanging out of the windows with guns drawn. I understood my body's limitations and conceded. I dropped sleepily, first to my right knee and then the other with my arms high above his head. The angry nationalists slipped out of the cars and immediately had five semi-automatics in harmony with my head. They had been yelling in Arabic since I was in ear shot and now they were slowing trading for broken English. One of the younger gunmen yelled, "You are American! You kill Hadi the greatest leader! You will die for this!"

An older leader calmed him and urged the others to back away from me. In a calmer voice he started giving me his sympathy. "You have done something very, very bad today". And with that he took the blunt end of his

162

rifle and swung a mighty strike into the side of my head. My body went bitter cold and blood fired out of my mouth. I fell unconscious again.

The five gunmen carried me into the back seat of the first car and made necessary calls over their cell phones. People had now begun to venture back into the streets. They easily understood war and violence after so many long years of hatred in their city. The first driver finished his call to the Prime Minister's office and motioned to start the caravan. Both Sedans pulled away from the crime scene just as a larger group of black vehicles showed up to calm the crowd and cover up most of the chaos.

The sedans ripped through the outskirts of Karkük as my body lied across a leather seat with a gun pointed at my head. After about 10 minutes through the intermingled streets of Karkük, my ears came into focus with my surroundings. I heard the driver talking on his cell phone. "We have him. He's in the back of our car and we're bringing him to the Embassy right away. We'll be there in 10 minutes."

I gained more consciousness from hearing this and wanted to open my eyes. The car hit a bump and a gun's cold, metal barrel tapped my forehead and I decided against it. For another couple minutes I began to think of my situation. The people who were driving me were a distinct police force of Hadi. I could tell by their faded gray police uniforms and pencil thin mustaches. I replayed the car bomb scene in my mind. My memory wrapped around the fact that whoever planned the bombing was extremely skilled in organizational

homicides. *These policemen are not responsible for this.*
Then I realized that the bombers had also failed at their
mission, because here I was, alive and well, in the back of
an average Iranian police cruiser. I began to hunt for any
indication of who might have carried out the explosion,
but before I could guess, my answer was thrown at me.

A large SUV peeled through an intersection and
slammed into the back, right side-panel of my sedan
causing both cars to explode with glass and debris. I
opened my eyes to see three men sliding out of the SUV
and interlocking stares with me. The driver of the SUV
gently tossed a hand grenade underneath the second
sedan. In my car, the two officers were slowly
recuperating and looked almost healthy just before they
were both shot in the temples by the men from the SUV.
The second car exploded. These men were Middle
Eastern, but wore dark suits and sunglasses. One of
them opened my door while the other two pried my body
out like a victim instead of a secret agent. Judging by the
way they calmly pulled me out of one car and placed me
into the other, told me that these were the men who killed
Hadi. These were the men who killed Mateo and Goose. I
stared down the men with frustration and fury, but I had
no strength to fight back. I wanted to see my enemies; I
wanted to learn the faces of and kill my enemies. So I
stared. I found myself boiling with confusion and anger,
and now pain from the concussions. The two handguns
pointed at my head were mocking my defenselessness.
The greatest spy in the world has been kidnapped. The
SUV shredded a trek of dust and shot down and out of

the city leaving 2 American spies, 5 Iranian officials, and 3 vehicles left for dead.

Nobody talked.

Nobody even breathed for 18 minutes, according to my watch that I was now comfortably looking at. The dark man in the passenger seat turned to me and began to answer my questions intuitively. His English accent was almost perfect; very little trace of the common Arabic-English I was so use to hearing. "My name is Masalu. You probably have no idea what is going on, so I will tell you. We, as you may have suspected, are members of The Masha'allah. I'm sure from your training that you know all about us, so we do not need to discuss our purpose here. What you don't know is why *you* are so important to us. The Masha'allah have been planning an overthrow of the Iranian government for some time now, but unlike many anti-nationalist groups in this area, we have been patient and smart about our choices. We only plot simple tasks, one at a time. Last night, two of our men managed to kill half of Hadi's staff at an auction in Qazvirt. This morning, Hadi entered his breakfast quarters to find the same two men tying down his wife and two daughters. Hadi was shot moments later.

"You are just common murderers, nothing more." I was furious with his political justifications. I, for the first time in a while, was ashamed of my profession. I had been killing government officials and double-agents for a year now, and finally the favor was being repaid, and it was disgusting. "Did you kill my friends, Masalu?"

"Unfortunately, yes," said Masalu with a depleting smile. "We only needed *you*; the others would have gotten in our way. I'm sorry for your loss. But I'm afraid that's the business we're in." Masalu now lifted the sunglasses down over his nose. I stared hard into his large, brown eyes with hatred. Masalu wiped a bead of sweat from his forehead and continued. "For years now, our leader has slowly been trying to win the hearts and money of American diplomats, but cannot. The Americans will not associate with us, because we are not unified. The nationalists were unified. They were under the thumb of the US government. We had no hope. But, now we have you, Frank, our most prized bargaining chip."

"I'm going to kill you for what you've done, Masalu."

Masalu paused for a second, glaring at me and slid his sunglasses back up the brim of his nose. "I'm afraid this is the extent of my introduction. Our leader is much crueler than you and I. I am sorry for the predicament you have fallen into." Masalu sighed and again turned to face the road in front of him. As he did, the two men in the back seat grasped my arms. With guns still aimed at my head, one man put a damp cloth over my nose and mouth. *Chloroform.*

17

There was an old television set speaking in the corner of a small room when I awoke. The room was a cage of cement block and steel bars and dirt. In the corner was I, face-first on the floor, half-asleep. The television was tuned to the only American-based news channel in the Persian Gulf. On now, was a female correspondent pressing a small device in one ear and describing her situation in a charming British accent. "Hadi was the 4th man inducted to the Global Weapons Board in and part of N.A.T.O's third tier missionary program. Here is a picture of him with former President Hallings this last May." The picture almost made me throw up at the thought of seeing this same man defiled by bullet holes only hours before.

Another man in a comfortable studio interrogated the woman. "Mary, could you please describe to the viewers what the scene around Karkük was just after the explosion?"

"Sure, Brent. The mothers immediately grabbed their children that were coming home from school and pushed them inside while the men grabbed the rest of their belongings from their carts in the streets. Most of the screaming was done by the children and stopped once their parents took them away. After that, it was actually quite calm here. From out of my balcony I could see dust and smoke mixing above the building we believe to be 421 Al-Qatar. This was a government office to our knowledge and served as the headquarters for some of Hadi's military operations. After a few moments, police sirens were heard from the inner part of the city. At this, more people began filing out of their homes cautiously."

"Could you see what was going on where the car exploded, Mary?"

"By the time I got down to street level, a larger crowd had formed around the vehicle and the police were trying to keep people away from the scene. They did not announce that Hadi was in the car. I found this out through a correspondent at the Embassy office downtown. So far, no new news has come to explain why any of this has happened. There is no word on who was responsible for the bombing, if the bombing was lead by a terrorist group, or if this was even really the Prime Minister in the car."

My eyes fluttered open and my head and arms hurt badly. My mouth and nose was filled with the terrible aftertaste of chloroform. It tasted like WD-40. I slowly grunted the strength to rock my body forward and sit up. I became very depressed when I realized the quick activities of the last few hours were not a dream. I had no perception of how long I had been asleep and a timid tan line is all that was visible on my left wrist where my watch had always sat. I looked around the room at the dirty concrete floor and the musty concrete walls and the dull steel bars. Then, I brought my focus back to the television.

"...and I don't expect any new news on the situation until then, Brent."

"So for those of you just joining us, there were a small series of car bombs in Karkük, Iran today. One of which was believed to be carrying the Prime Minister Khidir Hadi. Hadi was a very well-advised leader of the terrorist filled nation. During his three years in office, Hadi seized over 80% of the chemical weapons created during the Iraqi war, over 90% of the "Smart Bombs" from the Masha'allah terrorist group, and helped to all but eliminate the Guerilla forces in the Middle East. This is indeed an unfortunate turn of events for an area of the world plagued by war. The Republic of Iran's press secretary will make an official announcement later tonight to verify Hadi's death and to announce the upcoming steps to account for this tragedy."

I moved my stare back to the floor. I felt very cold and stale on the concrete. I was trapped and abandoned. Finally, I knew my luck had run out. I thought about Goose and Mateo. I thought about when I took this job a year ago. I thought about when I joined the Army. *Four years ago, I was much too innocent.* Then my mind began racing uncomfortably. I was hit by flashbacks from local news channels and government press conferences. I was blinded by the sight of prisoners of war being beaten in cold cells such as the one I was presently in. Slowly, I regained power over my fears and inhaled a long breath of sandy air.

I lifted up my body from the ground and felt the lump on the back of my head. It was a little bruised, but nothing a few Advil and time couldn't cure. I was performing a few harmless twists to rid the aches in my back when I heard a metal door slam down the hall. Barrages of *clacks* were created by a few sets of boots walking rapidly in my direction. My face turned to stone, and this time, Sir was screaming in my ear preparing me for a new fight. Three Masha'allah guards in turbans and suits stopped in front of the cell door. Keys from one man's pocket were fumbled and shoved into the cell lock. As the steel bar door opened, my heart was the only thing making noise.

Three guards entered into the cell and stared at me sternly. The guard on the right was by far the biggest while the others were merely giants. The middle guard cracked a smile, and with that, a fierce punch was thrown into my abdomen. My head was still hurting too much to concentrate and I took the blow with weakness. My upper body barreled over and the left guard swung an uppercut at my jaw. I saw this one coming and managed to get part of my hand in front to cushion the shot. I quickly backed away only to see the guards creep forward in unison. The right guard was holding a pair of shackles that quickly took residence with my left rib cage. I gasped for air, but was cut off by a final crack to the mouth. My upper lip was sliced and my nose was flooded, warm with blood. I crumbled down to the concrete floor. The guards all had a slightly bigger grimace on their faces now and moved in towards their prey. The two on the left took turns punting my rib cage while the right guard continued to pick me up and toss me down again. I succeeded at softening most of the major hits, but I was powerless over them all and my body was quickly rendered numb. The right guard took his final turn at stealing my breath with a hearty punch in the back of the head. One of the guards agreed that to be the last and the others followed him out of the cell, locking the steel behind them. The *clacks* moved swiftly away as I lay helpless in a heap.

I was in a fetal position for over an hour before I checked to see if the bleeding had stopped. There was a crimson puddle below where my head lay and a stream of sweat dripped from my hair. I managed to crawl into a kneeling position through a series of deep coughs. I was almost positive one or more of my ribs were broken. The nose had healed itself, but would remain weak for another day or two. I leaned my back up against the wall facing the steel bars and closed his eyes. Over and over, a voice was shouting in my ear, but not the Sir or Sergeant this time.

"Son, pain is an excuse for failure. There's no easier way to put it."

It was my father. I could see my dad in the backyard when I was 7, just before my parents died. My dad was teaching me boxing that day and I had just caught an accidental shot to the nose.

"Sorry boy. I thought you saw that one coming. Here, just suck it up your nose and spit it out. That is how you fight off pain, just get rid of the evidence."

7-year-old *me* attempted to suck up the filthy blood that was oozing onto my lips, but I couldn't take the hurt. My eyes welled up with salty tears and I ran into the house to get some towels and ice.

I took my gaze off of the bars and back to the blood on the floor. I took a deep breath and inhaled the rest of the warm blood in my nose and spit it into the corner.

For days I sat in that cell; that hard pit of stink on dust. Everyday became a similar routine. The lights in the hallway would turn on to startle me awake in the morning and they would go off at night leaving me in the uneasy silence. The guards outside my cell would not torture me, but if I got too cocky and insulted one of them, they wouldn't hesitate to knock me into place. No one spoke except me, usually to myself. There was a kinder bald guard that let me have a pad of paper to write on during the day. I wrote what had happened over the last few months and then I remembered what the man in the car, Masula, said on the way to this place. On the 10th day, I started going stir crazy with the thought.

"Masula! Has anyone seen Masula?!" The guards said nothing. "Hey you, baldy. Have you seen Masula?" Baldy didn't appreciate his new nickname and jammed his rifle into my kneecap. I didn't ask for Masula anymore.

On the 12th day, I got a word, two in fact, from the bald man. "Let's go," he grunted.

"Where are we going?" I asked. The bald man punched me in the stomach and politely repeated the two words again.

"Okay," I gasped.

We entered a long room. It was painted brown all the way down both walls and smelled like curry. There was a long table in the room with seemingly comfortable chairs. The bald man instructed me to sit in one. I sat and the man left the room. There was a clock on the wall, the first indication of time in days, other than the turning on and off of lights. I waited for thirty minutes or so before and noise entered the room.

The first person to enter was Masula. He was again wearing a perfectly gothic suit and appeared very clean. He sat down at the far end of the table without a word and opened a neat binder.

After a few more minutes the door opened again. Before anyone entered the room, Masula was standing and bowing his head. I remained in my comfortable seat. Then a man glided in that made my eyes explode with contrasting feeling. The man was American. He donned a light beard, short hair, and average street clothes. His eyes were glowing with pride. I looked over his wrinkled lines, his tan skin, his heavy eyebrows. He was the man from my third dream.

I shuttered when he spoke. "Frank, how are you doing?" I didn't answer. "Well, that's just peachy." Masula passed him the binder and the man began to read from it. "Enlisted 4 years ago...Trained in South Carolina...Moved up rank pretty quickly...Became First Team Sniper at 23...Hired by former president Jeffery Hallings at 24...Has killed 14 international politicians and weapons dealers. Not a bad record, Frank."

"I know you," I said to throw the man off guard, "I don't know how, but I know you."

"Yes you do, Frank. My name is Bernard Rush. I knew your mother. You were very young."

My mouth dropped open. This was not the answer I expected. It seemed the eight years I spent with my parents when they were alive was false, and the 16 years since had been my true childhood. Every corner was a brand new person with brand new secrets about my parents. All I wanted was an answer.

"You knew my mother? How? And what about my father?"

"Oh yes. I knew your father too, but I worked with your mother, so I knew him through her. Both extraordinary people, those two. It seems you've turned out much like them."

I was getting annoyed. "What is this Bernard? I've been beaten, deceived, my only two friends have been killed, and now you're trying to be buddy-buddy with me! If you're going to kill me, just do it already!"

"Kill you? Oh no, I have much more useful plans than that. And Goose and Mateo, they were just soldiers, Frank. You've got to put that behind you. What about your real friends?" he paused and became daring, "like Tom and Angela."

A rage was building up inside me. Bernard was getting cockier with every syllable. I bit my bottom lip and kept listening, trying not to reveal my emotions.

"Oh yes Frank, I know about Tom and Angela. I know almost everything about you in fact. I know your dorm room in college. I know where you worked. I know about the train incident. I know everything Frank. That's what I do."

"H-how? W-why?" I pleaded. And then, almost on cue, the door opened and another familiar face filled the room. It was Jeffery Hallings. My rage exploded and I dashed out of my seat and in a full sprint towards the man. Masula, who had yet to say a word, leaped over the table and snagged my collar in mid air. He yanked me to the ground and I threw a fist at his head. I connected with the edge of his skull, but not a clean enough shot to free me from his tight grasp. I looked forward and saw Bernard's boot drill me in the cheek bone. I blacked out.

When I became conscious, I was handcuffed to the chair and bleeding from my lip again. The former president and Bernard were talking and as I awoke, their words became clearer. Finally, I opened my eyes and Bernard gave me an "Ah, there he is. You know Frank, I didn't want to be this forceful with you. Thought you might cooperate. I guess there's more of your parents in you then we thought." I was too drowsy to speak, so I continued to listen.

President Hallings started. "I'm afraid I've been quite dishonest with you Frank," he smirked, "you were much smarter than I anticipated." His southern draw had a hint of laughter in it. "Son, let me tell you about the life you actually led. It started when you were very young. I was a senator then." My eyes gazed down the long table awaiting a most horrifying story. The president cleared his throat and began.

"In the early onset of the war in Iraq, I was a very young, very hungry politician. I was earning my seat in congress with money and I was determined to become a president for the same reason. Like any smart business man, I invested in weapons and oil when the promise of war came to America. I made a lot of money, in little time. But, I got carried away. I started gambling on the war. If one weapons company went down, another would pop back up in its place with me as the founder. Of course my name was never signed on any forms, but I had enough soldiers willing to put their reputation at stake for a few million dollars so I stayed rich.

After a few years, the war in Iraq was fading and became a social issue, not a political one. It was about to end and I had too much invested in it. I had other congressmen, CEOs, foreign diplomats all entrusting their money in me. I needed to keep my buyers happy. That's when it got out of hand. I issued the attack on Washington D.C. in the following months. I made the arrangements through ties I had with Bernard here. He was a leader in the Masha'allah group and a former US soldier. With the attack on Washington, Congress was sure to react. More troops were deployed, more ammunition was bought, and I made more money. The next year, I conquered my goal, and bought my ticket into the White House.

"Then, in the first months of my term, an interesting offer presented itself. Iran's newly crowned Prime Minister Khahir Hali asked me for financial help to defeat the Masha'allah. I graciously accepted and made it public for the world to see. I had one hand in the Iranian Republic and one hand in the Masha'allah. For the remainder of my term, I single-handedly fueled the American war. And I profited." The president took a sip of water and paused to phrase his next thought.

"Now about you Frank. It is quite curious how you came here today. Your parents had a friend. You knew him as Benny Angel, but he was in fact the first Wiseman, Tyler Robinson. Your father knew him from war. Tyler trained under your father. But, your father was not the cause of his death. No. It was your mother. What you don't know about your mother is that she worked for 15 years at the Department of Defense. A Special Forces Operator I believe was her title."

I almost choked knowing this. For years my mother would come home and put textbooks on the counter and tell me how rough the kids at school were that day. To me, she was a high school English teacher. She had lied.

"What I told you at my house was partially true. Tyler Robinson did become a rogue agent in Iran. Against me. He found out my secret while on a mission in Baghdad. The letter you wrote me was correct and I had him killed instantly. Unfortunately, it was not quick enough. By the time I got to him, he had released the information to Thomas Baylor, Daniel Finch, and ironically, your mother. He was a friend of hers from high school and he knew she worked at the DOD. He sent her a letter the day before his death and I traced it. My men set up wire taps in your parent's life right after that. Your house, their cars, their work. All under my supervision. Your parents knew a lot of important people and gathered up a group to discuss the letter. They were set to meet the night of the D.C. attack in the Archives Building."

My sides hurt and my eyes boiled with anger. I'm sure my face was a bright shade of cherry when the president said this.

"To say the least, I killed two birds with one stone that night. I rekindled a dying war and I eliminated all evidence pointing to me with the bombing, all except for Daniel Finch. He was by far the best agent when it came to disguising himself from the world. He disappeared and remained hidden for 12 years. I think he knew he never had enough evidence to prove anything, and by resurfacing, he would ultimately find his death.

"Then you came into the picture. We still had active taps on you for the remainder of your young life. We were afraid that your parents had left some kind of evidence for you when you became older. It never was true. But, when you came up on our radar as a new sharpshooter, the opportunity was too rich. We hired you to kill Daniel Finch, my last piece of evidence, and then we set you up, killing Goose and Mateo in the process."

The next words that came out of the president's mouth were chilling.

"You are the last person in the world who knows our secret, Frank."

I was numb again. "So what now? Are you going to kill me right here or make me wait a while?"

Bernard chimed in. "Actually, Frank, we're going to have you kill yourself, not on purpose of course." He was grinning a twisted grin.

"This is where it gets fun, Frank," said the president, "You're going to help us. See, the war is dying out again, and we need you to start up the fire. It's simple really. Tomorrow at noon, you are going to go on television and tell the world that you are a spy hired by the late Prime Minister Hadi. Word will surface and rumors will start spreading of a new attack against America and the failure of the military intelligence.

"After a week or two, when the fear of American society is at a peak, we strike. You are going to carry out the next great terrorist bombing on US soil. Congress will be forced to act. All over again, like a clock, the war begins. We will again put you on the air in front of millions of angry Americans and you will point the fingers of blame at Iranian government. Then, when the time is right, you will be tried and hung for treason."

The former president collected his thoughts.

"People think of war as a terrible, cold thing, Frank. But the truth is, war is necessary. From the struggle comes profit, from the killing comes life, from the loss comes gain. War is inevitable Frank; you're going to need to accept that for the weeks to come."

I was thinking icy thoughts when the president said this. I was trying to calm the shaking in my hands and stomach. I looked up to the cowardly leader and his accomplices. "But, what if I won't do it? I mean, what if I just kill myself before any of this goes through?" I was stern in my decision.

Bernard spoke. "We have a feeling you won't." He strutted out of the door and I heard muffled screaming. The screaming got louder and clearer as he came back into the room. He toted a live body with a bag over its head. Bernard removed the bag to reveal a much older, but nevertheless, beautiful Angela Pumpermyer. She was gagged and her hair was in a million directions. She had been crying for a long time. Her cheeks were flush with fear. I had seen those tears before. They made a pit in the bottom of my stomach.

I tried breaking the handcuffs when I realized who it was. But, instead I just badly bruised my wrists, over and over. I continued trying until my head eased my heart. I slumped back in my seat and began to cry. It was the first time in years.

18

Angela and I were dragged and forced into our cells.
Hers was adjacent to mine. We sat with our backs to the
concrete dividing us and listened to our breathing
through the bars. She didn't speak for hours. Just
sobbing and tears. I spent the time daydreaming. I was
alone again in my old brown chair.

In my empty mind, I was a speed skater poising on
the starting line to wait for an inevitable gunshot. *Bang!*
My skin tight suit and my blades of sharp metal took off
in a flash. I hustled around the first turn and quickly
took my place gently behind the favored contender. He
was a Korean with smooth maneuvers and razors for
skates. With each push I heard a *zzziii zzziii zzziii*. I
drafted behind the Korean for three laps and mimicked
his grace.

The Olympic cheers were getting louder and louder as we sprinted into the final laps. At every turn, the Korean leaned into a perfect semi-circle and then jetted into a straight sprint. While in the turns, he would calmly cross his feet over each other, hiding the power and pressure in each step. With time running out, I took my chance. At two laps left, I felt my body break free from the Korean. My right foot took a quicker kick in the turn and my left foot followed. I skirted through the inside of the Korean and found an extra half step that he didn't have. I pushed on each leg with a gigantic thrust and moved into position. On the next turn, the Korean went for the same move and succeeded. We came into the final turn neck and neck. As I jutted my front leg out at the finish line, I woke up to the sound of Angela's voice. She was done crying.

"Frank?"

"Yea."

"How are you?" She always was the compassionate one.

For the next few hours, we talked like old friends whose lives had been separated in a twisted psychology experiment. I told her about how I joined the army after the subway incident and had been a rifleman, a secret agent, and now a scapegoat. The way I presented my story was bleak and draining, not near as exciting as I had once thought it. The deaths of Goose and Mateo had created a completely negative ending to the last few years of my life.

Angela's story was much more cheerful. Just like when we were together, she always seemed to find a brighter side. After me, she found love in a student at Georgetown. They got married two years later and he was now a partner at a D.C. law firm. I fell silent when she said, "I had a baby 4 months ago, Frank."

After a few moments of breathing, I told her, "It's going to be okay Angela, I promise." Then, I retreated to the back corner of my cell and fell asleep to unreachable hopes. When I awoke a bearded man was standing next to me. It was God.

"*Now* you show up," I grimaced sarcastically. "Where were you when I was getting into all of this mess? Huh?"

"Frank, I'm not here to argue. You still remember your dream, right?"

"Well, yea. Yea, I remember it. The one where I save the world?"

"That's the one. It is important that you remember that dream Frank, exactly as it happened. A lot of people are counting on you."

I had a concerned look on my face. "Why? Am I really going to save the world God? God?"

He walked out of the cell without saying anything else. My voice had woken up Angela.

"Frank, is that you? What are you saying?"

I looked towards the empty space where God had stood. "Nothing," I said.

My dream *was* still very fresh in my head. The scene, the people, the bright red switch. I fought hard through it looking for something more glaring, more obvious. Nothing. I came out of the dream with the same level of vagueness I had when I was twenty years old.

Angela was calling through the metal bars. "Frank? What are we going to do?"

I thought about what God had told me. I thought about how president Hallings' and Bernard's plans unraveled. For once, I knew the exact answer to Angela's question.

"We're going to do exactly what they want."

"Frank, they're going to kill you. You heard them. Please, just mess up their plan or something. You know, expose Hallings for the scumbag he really is. I would be selfish if I said I would rather save my life than save all the innocent people that are going to be killed in the next few years over this." She remained determined in her speech although hints of doubt and sadness could be heard throughout the dusty hallways. "Please Frank, I'll be okay."

I knew she was talking about heaven when she said this. She was always better at that than me. I would go to church and read and learn and pray, but I always had doubt. There were always questions in my voice. Angela just knew.

I leaned into the cold metal bars as far as my skin would let me. "Angela," I started, "You're going to be fine." She did not speak after this. I could hear her start crying again.

19

It was 8:21 am when I was lashed from my cell and carried away to The Shywater. The Shywater was an American-owned resort located in the heart of Tehran, Iran, the capital city. Popular diplomats and billionaires frequented this resort everyday for peace from the outside world.

We flew into the city with an ease I hadn't felt on a plane in years. Tehran was different than the sand-filled wastelands that were tossed about on American media channels with bombs and blood. The city was not as tall as American cities, but equally as large. The buildings alternated between standard rectangular boxes and elegant skyscrapers designed for beauty as much as function. The roads leading into the center were a cardiovascular system of black, winding veins. Along the sides was luscious foliage, ripe with colorful spurts of life.

Behind the city were blue and white mountains that reached higher than the clouds. Their tips were rough and frosted, but cascaded down into mellower, richer land. Just before the mountain reached the busy city, a barricade of farms and rural life held the two apart. From inside the plane, I could almost taste the warm air and prosperity of such a bold metropolis. It struck me dumb that I would be traveling here as a prisoner. I began to shake again.

On the flight over, the former president gave me my script. It was full of lies and darkness, but I obliged. Immediately off the plane, I was handcuffed and dragged into another black Escalade similar to the one I was laying unconscious in a week ago. Inside were Masula, Bernard, and two other darkly dressed members of Masha'Allah. The former president rode in another car.

We arrived to the front gate of the resort a little after 11 am Tehran time. The US was still sleeping. As we pulled in towards the entrance, I spotted the US Embassy to the left. It was a rather plain building compared to the grandeur of The Shywater. Another dark suit opened the door for Bernard and me. He knew Bernard and said, "The press is here just like you said sir. They are all in the conference room or around at the front."

I had been mistaken in thinking the elegant entrance we arrived at was the front. In fact, our entrance seemed unkempt when compared to the front of the resort. I peered through a hedge when crossing into the hotel and caught a glimpse of the front garden. There were roses hanging from vines that covered contemporary art. The stairs were as white as ivory and equally grand. I managed to see a few dozen reporters standing outside just before I was yanked by my cuffs into an empty parlor.

The man who let us out of the car led us through a desolate pattern of hallways and staircases. The floor was crimson and the walls were gold. I could hear a buzzing in the walls as we got closer to our destination. Finally, we marched up a narrow set of stairs and the buzzing engulfed my head. We seemed to be backstage of a theatre of some sort. I turned to ask Bernard where we were. He nervously said, "This is called the Iranian Conference Room, not a good translation I'm afraid. This is where every main piece of legislation and news bulletin is created in this area. On most days, Iranian diplomats are the only people allowed in this theatre. Not today." Bernard started lifting material out of boxes and handing them to all of the men. "Today we, the Masha'Allah, will have the floor. And today the Iranian, and American, and British news heroes will only listen. Today, we will make the world recognize *our* power."

When he said this, his eyes were on mine with red anger. His breathing had greatly increased, but he was no longer nervous, he was daring. He handed me a bullet proof vest.

"Here. You might need this."

Curiously, I peeked through the curtains behind the stage. I started at the top, recognizing many famous military leaders and American diplomats. President

Hallings was in the middle talking to the Secretary of the State. I slowly lowered my gaze down to the mezzanine level where Iranian officials were gathering in their important blue suits. Finally, my eyes dropped down into the panic that was in front of the stage. I found the source of the buzzing.

There must have been two thousand or more journalists, wearing all different badges, yelling all different languages, and wondering, without patience, what was about to happen. If Jesus saw this many people waiting for him at Mt. Sinai, he might call it a gathering, or even a congregation. But I was not Jesus. This was a slew.

My eyes were wide in fear when Bernard tapped me on the back and told me it was time. I felt a lump in my throat disappear into my stomach and I paced slowly after Bernard. He motioned for me to wait in a spot behind the curtain and he slid through the slit. I heard the buzzing calm down to a dull murmur and then vanish to silence when Bernard approached the podium. His nervousness was gone. From the muffled material of the curtain I could hear Bernard begin. His dark suited men behind me were bowing their heads as if in prayer.

"Good morning ladies and gentlemen," started Bernard. "Today is a day of subtle realization in the world. I am a general of the Masha'Allah." Noise again filled the room and hatred could be felt in the air. Slowly the noise fell and I imagined Bernard was holding up his hands to silence the slew. Again he spoke.

"For many years now, you, the Iranian government, have pursued and massacred our people to limitless ends.

We have had no place to call our own, no land to claim, and yet we have survived on our will to fight and our right to live in this country as much as you do. Until now we have been shy about making accusations against your people, but we can wait no longer." The room was dead silent and Bernard took his time. "Your former leader, Khadir Hadi was gunned down by our men two weeks ago." The crowd erupted out of silence and started shouting curses towards Bernard. He shouted over the mob and finished his point. "We didn't intend to kill Hadi! That was an accident! It was an accident!" Many journalists hushed the Iranian officials so they could hear the stern man. "But, we did complete our mission. We captured an internal spy on Hadi's force. The man is here today and has a few statements he would like to make. I think you will be interested to hear what he has to say."

Through the curtain, Bernard made a scooping motion telling me to come out. I took my last breath of an honest life and swam through the slit in the curtain into the depths of the theatre. The slew was even more massive up close. Thousands of glaring eyes were burning into mine. I crept to the podium and the only noise to be heard was the clicking of camera flashes. I pulled out the paper that the former president had written and spoke into the metallic microphone.

"Hello. Three years ago I was a rifle scout in the US Army. After a mission in Baghdad, an officer who worked close with Prime Minister Hadi approached me about an interesting job opportunity. I was to become a spy for the Iranian government. With the money put forward by

Hadi, I graciously accepted the offer. For the next few years, I sold secrets to the late president while continuing to work for the army. I left the military when my major gained suspicion that I was trading secrets. I returned to Hadi and continued to work as a special agent."

Everything I said was lifeless and calm. My words were just scratches on a page. There was no emphasis behind them and I never looked off the paper.

"In my time with Hadi, I learned of many illegal operations he was a part of. Namely, the Washington D.C. attacks more than a decade ago. He also has been stealing money from the US Treasury. He requests more funding for medical aid and turns around and uses the money for weapons and investments. He built a stronger government at the cost of the Iranian people."

I slowed down and took a deep breath. The crowd was starting to stir again with my accusations.

"I've compiled a set of documents at the threat of the Masha'Allah providing proof of the allegations I am making today. In the documents, you will find the timeline of Hadi's transactions with US legislatures, timesheets that directly coordinate with the D.C. attack, and a list of Hadi's assistants in this attack, many who are still in office today. You will also find a list of people not associated with Hadi's regime including former and current US presidents and members of the Masha'Allah. This attack was done solely by the Iranian government under Hadi's rule."

The next line of the page was staring harshly at me as I gazed into the microphone. "I am a prisoner of war. The Masha'Allah asks that the United States pay two million dollars for my safe return or I will be executed on October 21st at dawn."

I took one final look at the page and turned and walked from the podium. The slew exploded into yelling and fighting. American reporters were shoving Iranian newsmen, and an entire balcony of Iranian officials was on its feet and spitting harsh words in my direction. I was two feet from the curtain when it hit me in the side. *Phap!* A quick bullet drilled me in the vest and I fell to the stage with a numb tingling. Before I could tell what happened, another gunshot echoed in the great hall and Bernard was pulling me by my collar off the stage. I took a quick glance back at the mass hysteria that was The Shywater Slew.

20

Bernard carried my numb body all the way out of the resort and into the Escalade. The other men with dark suits followed behind taking warning shots at any aggressive onlookers. We quickly crammed into the SUV and peeled out of the elegant driveway. Pebbles kicked and tires sped out of the city in blinding speed. No one talked much, except for Bernard, who gave short directions to the driver. After fifteen minutes, Bernard helped me out of my vest and looked at my side. It was navy blue and already sore. I cringed when he laid a bag of ice on it.

A few dozen miles out of the city, the Escalade swerved onto a dusty path. We were again back into the part of the Middle East that I knew too well. The sand, the hot, the dead. In the distance, a helicopter was landing and making miniature tornados dance along the vacant floor. As the Escalade came to a stop, Bernard gave me an apologetic look and clasped the handcuffs on me again. Only he and I entered the chopper and the other men retreated in the car.

We accelerated upward into a red-orange sky. After a few hours, we were back to the fortress. I had paid close attention when leaving that morning and returning that evening to the direction of our trip. But by the lack of effort by Bernard to keep the location a secret, I could tell he no longer cared. I could estimate that we were roughly 400 miles southwest of the capital which would put us on the Iraqi side of the Iran-Iraq border. Wherever we were, it was clear nobody else was in the area. Only strong sand winds and the occasional lightning storms gave this barren land excitement.

Bernard dragged me back into the residence, which was beginning to remind me of a Navajo pueblo in New Mexico, without the pride. We clamored down a steel flight of stairs and into the hallway of jail cells. They were just as we had left, completely empty save for a dismal Angela leaning on the bars.

I was handed over to the bald guard who removed my shackles and pushed me into the concrete tank. Just as Bernard was leaving the hall he shouted "Turn on the TV Frank!"

"What channel?!" I yelled back. There was no answer. The bald guard turned to me and spoke.

"Any channel."

I did as I was told. The TV came on and there I was in faded color. The news reporter was chiding wildly.

"This is a soldier who deserted, who deceived...no, there is no reason why we should spend taxpayer's money to retrieve him from the situation he has fallen into. This is a mistake he has made."

"She's kind of snotty," I commented to myself. I changed the channel and saw another face of me with Arabic subtitles flashing on my body. The guard was right, I was on every channel and each had its own twist on the situation.

"Frank," said Angela softly, "I was thinking today, you know, about dying. And I don't think that..."

Before she could say anymore a latch at the end of the hall opened and in stammered Bernard.

"Get him out of there."

I was led into another dark room in the underground establishment. This room was wider than the other with a single window in the top corner leaking casual sunlight into the eerie grayness. Bernard sat me down at a cold steel table with my wrists cuffed in front of my stomach. Their timing was getting too crucial to have me lash out at them again, so they did not take anymore chances.

Bernard walked across the room to a manila filing cabinet and pulled out a roll of large paper. He laid the paper in front of me, unrolled it, and weighted it down on the edges of the table. The paper was a blueprint. As I scanned in more detail, I saw it was a blueprint of an Iranian Missile Facility. Bernard rushed back into the room. He had already started talking before he entered. "This is what we've been training you for, Frank."

"Excuse me?" I said a little startled at the quick entrance of noise backing into my life.

"This is your final mission, these blueprints. Right here." He pointed to a box on the blueprints with the words "Prisoner Cell" in drafting letters. "This is where you are going to be at 4:00 pm tomorrow."

I skimmed over the document at the odd angles and boring text. I had seen a million of drafts just like this in college, and at the same time, I hadn't seen any. This was not a simple drawing today, it was my destiny. I ran my finger over the word Prisoner Cell one more time and followed the print to the next page where, just above the cell, on the second floor, was a custodial closet. Like a rat catching the scent of warm cheese, my cuffed hand dragged along the ink, out of the closet and down a hallway. Bernard stood over me with exceptional ego. His plan was becoming reality in both of our minds.

The hallway led to nowhere in particular, passing rooms marked Conference or Media. I flipped the page to what was labeled as the third floor. The third floor was more promising. Above one of the conference rooms was another custodial closet, and then, nothing. The hallway coming from the closet led to four more rooms, but none of them had names. Bernard had scribbled his own words in one of the rooms. *Control room.* The words were circled in red ink.

My head was piecing together the images in the blueprint. "You want me to get there, don't you?" I asked a very anxious Bernard.

"Yes, Frank. This is what we've been training you for. You came to us as a sharpshooter. That was what we *needed*. But what we *wanted* was a man with no background, no face that would be missed if erased. The missions we sent you on in the last year were hardly necessary except for the training it gave you. Every mission was different. We gave you everything from lessons in explosives, missions that required quick actions, and ones that were stealthy and quiet.

"With your shooting skills, we knew you'd have something to fall back on if you ever got into trouble. You were the perfect candidate. The mission tomorrow is going to require you to use every piece of knowledge you've learned in the last year. Because of this, we have an incentive for you.

"For your final mission with us, we will give you your life." Bernard was almost smiling his wicked smile that he kept close for times like this.

"And Angela's life?" I said.

"Of course, Frank. She's got a plane ticket home tomorrow night in fact. You... not so much. You will keep your life, but it will be something different." Bernard handed me a passport with my picture and a new name.

"Benny Angel," I sighed.

"The one and only," assured Bernard. "After this mission, we'll send you to somewhere remote, Columbia or Russia perhaps, and after that, you're life is what you make of it."

I was overwhelmed with gladness, but was quickly dragged back into depression. I was selling my soul. Many people were going to die for my selfishness. All I could hear in my mind was the president saying "War is inevitable" and scrambled sounds of the American reporters condemning me at The Shywater. I had become a very real vagabond among two nations. I bowed my head in sorrow.

"Frank, tomorrow will be just another day, just another mission. Are you ready?"

"Yes." And we began the meeting.

The building's infrastructure was much more complicated than I had seen at first glance. The corridors and oddly sized rooms had no real flow or consistency. Tomorrow at noon, I would be escorted and banished into the Prison Cell on the ground floor of the Iranian Security Council. Elected members of the Middle East Treaty Organization would be collaborating that afternoon in the main room of the building. Among them would be former president Hallings, the council of Iranian diplomats, and members of the Masha'Allah. They would be discussing the allegations set against former Prime Minister Hadi, the terms broken in the Iranian peace treaty, and eventually and less importantly, me.

In the cell, I would be heavily guarded by a member of each party represented at the meeting. Bernard represented The Masha'Allah. I gathered from Bernard that this would be to ensure full protection from any outside group wanting to kill me.

While listening to Bernard talk about the stances of each party, I realized this; the United States wanted me dead for selling secrets to Iran, the Iranians wanted me dead for selling out their president, and Bernard and President Hallings wanted me dead for knowing everything, but needed me for another few hours first. So it goes.

The plan would start before I even entered the cell. Bernard would enter the building with two syringes hidden under his pant leg just above his ankle. Also, since we had to pass through a metal detector in almost every room, a small plastic tube was stuffed in Bernard's coat pocket. Just after two o'clock, Bernard would act first.

I could see the sweat dripping over my bangs. The cell was hot and damp. No cameras, no air conditioning. The cell was a horrific example that this part of the world was slow to move. For the first few hours, I sat with my head down in the corner running over the plan in my head, perfecting the outcome. When Bernard struck, I was no further along in my planning than when I had started.

There would be a bench outside of the cell in which the three guards would sit and wait and watch. They would not talk and not move. Bernard would strike before either knew what hit him. By faking an itch, Bernard would draw the tiny syringes from his ankles and thrash them into the two brutes. The poison in the needles was not deadly, just a simple numbing solution. The poison would run through the bodies of the guards so quickly that by the time they got their hands around Bernard's throat, their arms would be limp. They're mouths would run dry and gasp for air, and they would fall unconscious.

I picked my head up from my stare into the floor when I heard Bernard strike. He was quick and curt in his motions. The men were on both sides of him and he pulled up the syringes and drilled them in the chests. The Iranian guard immediately gasped and pulled out the needle, holding onto his ribs. The Marine was a little less concerned about his own well-being and swung a hand into Bernard's throat. The Marine squeezed harder and harder to cut Bernard's breath, but dizziness came across him quickly leaving his hands falling under their own weight.

When both were unconscious, Bernard leaned their bodies up against his own and forced their heads into an upright position. Neither guard made a motion to yell for help when the poisoning occurred, but the clashing of bodies echoed down the hall. Another guard at a post around the corner peeked his head in to see if any new action had occurred. He stared at me with my head down again, he stared at the three guards, still sitting humbly on the bench, and he turned back to his post.

Bernard would then throw me the plastic tube from his jacket and continue to sit patiently. The rest would be my job. I would start with the ceiling. The tube contained an acidic gel that would eat through most of the material. With one hand on a cement block on the ceiling, and one hand holding the bottle, I would spread the gel into the crevices of the block containing a caulk.

The cell reminded me of the cell that Bernard kept me in. It was dusty and concrete, but it served a purpose. As I began putting the acid onto the caulk, I wondered if the men that had built this prison saw me destroying it, they would applaud or be furious. I assumed furious and kept gelling. After a few minutes, small bubbles formed on the outside of the concrete tile and the caulk was disappearing and leaking to the floor below.

After the block was removed, I would use it as step and hoist myself into the ceiling leaving the cell behind. From there, Bernard would remain sitting and I would move as fast as possible. Bernard would not see me for 30 minutes at least, but he was confident that Angela's life was too important to me. In a way, he would trust his own life in mine.

I pulled myself into the ceiling with difficulty. The bruise from yesterday's bullet was at its peak of pain and every movement of my torso brought a shiver through my core. Inside the ceiling was pitch black and this is where my memory of the blueprint came in handy.

Next, I would make my passage through the duct work of the ceiling. I would have five rooms to crawl over and no flashlight to navigate. From the cell, I had mapped out in my head the blueprint and the path I would take. I would make an immediate left and continue through ten sets of main frames. The main frames of the building would have larger metal brackets than the support frames and require me to crunch to the diameter of a basketball. The time spent in the mattress hunting Daniel Finch would help me cope with the claustrophobia. In the tight metal brackets of the building's ribcage, I would wait.

At the instant the sound of the cell disappeared and I headed into an echo of metal and concrete, my breath stopped. I slunk like a scorpion through the duct work with no noise and no slips. My steps were gently cautious and my eyes were twitching like fireflies looking for potential snags. As I crept across the brackets, I could hear people scuffling above me. An occasional laugh or shout would startle me and send my heart racing. The racing would make noise in my chest and again I would have to settle my mind and calm my nerves. Finally, I made the trek to the fifth room and I felt the patience sink in.

In the ceiling's rafters, I would listen above to the common workers in blue talking in an Iranian slang. I would wait here until the stammering stopped. When it did, I would make a right turn and slide into position next to a floor-level air vent on the second floor. Through the air vent was my escape into much more space and fresh air. Slowly and quietly, I would unfasten the screws on the air vent and place the metal bracket onto its side. With one more check for movement, I would squeeze my body through the vent and into the custodial room. My next step would be done.

I waited for 45 minutes before I heard the workers leave the room. They were watching a scrambled television in the corner that was reporting on the events occurring one the floor below me. I had a grin on my face that said, "If they only knew". As I waited for the broadcast to end, I could feel my legs start to cramp up and my back shake in the awkward pressure it was taking. Finally, the goons left the room at the sound of their boss cursing in Iranian. They shut down the television and hopped out of the room, slamming the door behind them. I could smell the fresh air in the vent and I slid quickly to my gateway. Frantically, with a feeling like after a long car trip, I bursted through the hatch and sent the metal swinging onto the loud concrete floor. The echo startled me and I waited to see if anyone else had heard it. No one came. I put both hands on the sides of the vent and hoisted my body through the tiny, sharp opening. The edges cut my shirt and dug into my skin above my bruise from yesterday's shooting. A small puddle of blood formed on my shirt, but it was harmless. I stood up in the custodial room and went back to my task.

After making it to the second floor, I would begin the combatant part of the mission. Carefully, I would open the door to the custodial room and proceed down the hall in front of me, four more doors on the left. There was no way to know who would be in this hallway, under what supervision, and with what weaponry, but I had none and would have to make due in whatever situation. Bernard had studied surveillance tapes he had made from a building across the street, but the long range camera could only begin to peek in at the mysterious hallway that would await me. At the fourth door, I would use a tool from the custodial room and pick the lock.

Before I left the custodial room, I grabbed a pair of pliers and a very small screwdriver. Then, I opened the door not knowing what would be waiting my arrival. Emptiness. I slowly creaked the door open more and more, but there was no one or nothing in sight. The halls were barren and plain. I didn't hesitate. I dashed to the fourth door on the left and felt the knob. It was loose.

The knob turned and I was shocked to find it was unlocked. Just as I barged myself through the door, two sets of amazed, dark eyes caught mine. They were sitting in plush chairs, drinking a cola, and watching the news. By the first impression, these were the two men in the custodial closet. They were round and sluggish in their reaction to my entry. I could tell by the way they were startled at first, that they thought I was their boss. After a second glance, they decided otherwise but quickly found a worse conclusion. The larger man took a quick look at the television and saw me staring back at him. My fighting instincts from PT kicked in. The larger man turned to find his meeker friend already badly struck in the chin and falling to the floor. He looked to me just in time for an equally heavy blow that sent him into a dense state. I drew two final shots into the men collarbones and tied their sagging bodies up to the table. They fell into a short term coma.

After I made it safely into the conference room, I would need to get moving faster. Chances of anyone seeing me would now be increasing exponentially and any unusual actions in the building would be enough to cause an immediate dog hunt. Next, I would be going into the ceiling once more. I was still a floor away from my destination.

Quickly, I hopped onto the middle of the table and began applying the bottle to the concrete ceiling. The potion wasn't working quite fast enough for my heart. Finally, the concrete lost its strength and fell into my arms. I slid the block over into the corner with the lifeless men and returned to the table. Like an athlete, I shot up into the ceiling and began my crawl down the length of the building. I remembered back to my race at the train station. I didn't look back for a second.

In the ceiling, I would be moving at a quick pace four rooms down. I would have to make sure to keep moving at all costs in case someone did hear me from below and start firing shots into the ceiling. I would eventually make it to the fourth room where I would slink up into another custodial closet. This one would be smaller and, most likely, vacant. From there, I would begin my final sprint.

My heart was racing and I thought back to my daydream of the speed skater. I felt the dusty air from the vents blowing past my ears. The metal and concrete were sharp on every move, but I kept my pace using each nook as a starting block to propel forward. I pulled with my arms and kicked with my legs, each crawl was more uncomfortable than the next. Finally, I made it to the fourth room. Again, I took a look at the air vent and began to scurry. With less precision than the last vent, I turned my body and booted it open sending loud metal pieces flying across the floor. The vent itself twanged against the ground and I slid on through. There were no lights on and I searched for a switch. When the lamp blink on, I saw a barren closet with an empty filing cabinet and one lunch box on top of it; most likely a worker's. I peered inside the lunch box and found a banana, a half eaten sandwich, and a loaded gun. Tension had been high in this building for the last few days so I almost didn't even flinch when I saw the weapon lying there. I picked it up and threw it into the back of my pants, tucked into my waist.

The whole time I would be climbing through the building, Bernard would be sitting on the bench with his unconscious friends waiting for my safe return. We never really had a second plan in case anything went wrong. It just seemed natural that a veteran killer, like Bernard, and a veteran spy, like me, could handle ourselves under pressure. After arriving in the closet, I would have one final run. I would make a dead sprint to a room down the hall labeled 302. This was the Control Room.

In the Control Room was the database for a small missile launch site outside of Baghdad. The database was easily accessible thanks to a friend of the former president's. This is where the help from the Explosives Team would come into play. On the long trip from Saudi Arabia to Ahvaz, the Explosives Team talked about women, killing, and missiles. They didn't speak to me directly, but I heard everything they said. They talked about trajectory, launch codes, and ignition sets.

Bernard gave me a crash course on the missile launch program I would be using before we left. I listened intently pretending this was the first time I had heard the lecture when in fact the Explosives Team had already given me all the information and more. I didn't tell Bernard.

I had just finished stuffing the gun into the back of my pants when I heard three gun shots that vibrated the walls. The shots were distant, but still caught my breath. In a panic, I opened the door of the closet and took off running down the hall. There was no one in the hall and

I stopped in front of room 302. A keypad was in front of me and I began to enter the code the president recited to me. As I tapped in the second number, two more gunshots rang out through the building and sounded closer than before. Loud clomping could be heard in the distance of the long hall.

Before long, the noise was on top of me and my heart beat like a drum. Just then, Bernard swung around the corner with a gun swinging at his hip. He was bleeding at the leg and had a casual limp as he ran. He saw me and screamed, "Frank! Get in the room!" I quickly started reentering the password when I heard shots from another party come whizzing into the hallway. Glass shattered everywhere when one struck a cabinet. The password was entered, the door opened and Bernard limped toward me just in time. He turned to fire two more shots at his chasers and I pulled him into the room.

21

There we were, Bernard and I, in the most powerful room in the Middle East. For a second, all seemed calm and still in the world. The silence was broken by a case of gun shots striking the door and sending echoes through the room. My ears rang into a high pitch scream and I lost most of my hearing. Bernard yelled curses and fell to the floor grabbing his bleeding leg. He pulled on my shoulder and mouthed words. "Go launch the missile! I'll hold these guys off!"

I showed my force. "No! First let Angela go!"

"What?!" he said half not hearing and half not understanding.

"Call your men and tell them to let Angela go then I'll program the missile!"

"Fine!" Bernard started dialing just as the door was broken open and live bullets filled the room. Bernard shot through the bottom crack in the door wounding one of the men. He fell to the floor and the door was slammed shut again. Bernard continued to dial. "Hello, Masula? It's me, Bernard! Release the girl, Angela, just let her go!" A pause. "No, don't follow her", he said as he looked up at me, "we've completed the mission!"

It was strange, but I didn't even feel like I need to check the phone to make sure Bernard had actually called. Throughout the last few weeks a unique bond of hatred had formed between Bernard and me. Although we both wanted different things, we also could both recognize the other's abilities. His abilities were pure evil, yet grand.

I nodded and turned to sweep towards the database. Just then, another round of snapping bullets came jutting through the room when the door cracked open. I watched as Bernard was struck again in the leg and he bellowed in pain. I crept around the corner to avoid the shooting and I stopped cold.

This was it. This was my dream. I stared fondly at the red and blue wires hanging down around the metal dividers. I reached out and touched them to make sure they were real. My ears seemed to have gone deafer as I carefully sauntered down the aisle. I stopped at each opening to make sure there were no shots flying by me.

I crept up to the control panel in awe of its eternal glory. The buttons were all I had seen in my mind for the last six years. So much had change since then, it was hard to believe this is how I ended up in this peculiar situation. The world slowed down for the next few minutes.

Without hesitation, I started to carefully adjust the control panel. The buttons were blinking and a screen with block print numbers was scrolling in green font.

I thought about my life over the last few weeks, how I had given in to the torture, the pain, and most of all, the acceptance of failure.

I began to adjust the trajectory of a Series 1 attack on the United States' eastern seaboard.

I thought about my career in the Army brought about by luck and manipulation. I was ashamed of the path I chose, I was ashamed of the betrayal I was setting.

The green font screen began asking me for commands and I responded diligently. The launch codes, the program, the ultimate destination to initiate a missile attack on the United States. Lives would be lost and the cycle of war would again restart, just like the president had said.

My focus shifted and I smiled when I thought of Angela going home to her child. I smiled when I thought of Tom and me eating Chinese food. I smiled at my grandmother taking me to church.

The database ran the codes perfectly. The numbers skid through the machine and one final command was printed on the screen. ACTIVATE LAUNCH.

My parents were in my ear. "Frank," they said, "we're so proud of you." I felt my hand drifting towards the red blinking switch in the corner of the panel. It was all that was left to do. And then, out of the bullets, and war, and crunching metal, Bernard spoke.

"Go ahead Frank, you're about to save the world."
His words were cold and sarcastic. I turned around to
see the, once strong man, reduced to a heap of clothes
and skin on the floor. Blood was smeared from his waist
down and hand prints were tainted on all of the wires.
His gun was drawn on me as a reminder to complete my
task. When I had the dream of this moment, Bernard
was larger, more powerful to me. Now he was a sniveling
rat. There seemed no reason to be scared of him. He was
a fallen man.

As I stared blankly at Bernard, I imagined what it
felt to be innocent again. I thought back to the first time I
fired my grandfather's rifle. I thought back to the train
ride and how quickly I fought off the gunmen. I thought
back to the day Goose died. The bomb counting down the
seconds in the car. The way I turned and leapt just in
enough time to be alive today. These incidents had
shaped my life, and as I stood there over a pitiful man, a
familiar feeling graced my soul. With my history in mind,
I reacted.

I pressed the blinking red button and the screen
printed back LAUNCH ACTIVATED. Bernard saw the
successful words and lowered his weapon. At this, I
pulled the gun from my back and put a shot into
Bernard's head. I stood there for a few seconds with a
posture like John Wayne. The door busted open and
shouting and ammunition ricocheted off the walls. I
tucked the gun into my pants and I got down on the floor
in a prayer position. In the best Arabic I could muster, I
shouted "I'm over here. I've killed him."

The men immediately saw me and approached with discomfort. They were very slow to move and even more quiet. They ran their eyes over the mess of the room. Blood was smeared on everything and leading up to a dead man with a hole in his head. In front of him was a kneeling man with clean hands in the air. Behind him was a missile launch system with horrifying words scrolling across the screen.

The oldest man in the group approached me and asked with great concern, "D-did you launch a missile?"

I looked up at the man. He had fear in his brow. It was obvious he had a family and even more obvious he was tired of deaths in his country. I calmly looked up to the man and told him, "No sir. I stopped *him* from launching one."

The man's eyes released their tension and he shifted me to my feet. He was just forceful enough to tell me that he was vulnerable, but gentle enough to say "thank you". With no order at all, the men helped escort me out of the Control Room and down to the first floor.

The building was empty as we made our way through the hallways and conference rooms. One of the guards explained that the diplomats had been filed out of the building as soon as news spread that I had escaped. I took one last look at the entrance room with the golden desks and the chandelier clad ceilings. It was beautiful in a very odd way.

The older guard, with a grip on the scruff of my neck, shadowed me out into the street. As we sifted through the golden doors, a crowd erupted. Cameramen and news reporters were everywhere being held back by

Iranian policemen. They had taped off an area of the street for the diplomats and the building employees. I walked slowly down the marble stairs towards ground level with the mass of people. As I walked, the older guard got closer and closer to me, like a shield. He, as well as I, could feel just as many cold eyes on me as there were confused ones. I said a silent prayer as I crept down, that no one would fire a shot at me just yet. It wasn't my time.

With prayer answered, I made it to the bottom of the steps. The older guard took control of the situation as best he could. He raised a megaphone handed to him by another guard and clicked the switch.

"Ladies and gentlemen, today a man tried to initiate an attack against the United States. That man is now dead in the control room, six feet from the launch panel. This young man right here," he said while draping an arm over my shoulder, "killed that man. Thanks to you," now talking directly to me, "a ray of sun has shown through our dark clouds of war. It is not my job to release anymore information as of right now, but I'm sure a press conference will be held later in the evening."

The second he finished, the crowd again erupted in chatter. Over the noise, the diplomats found a reason to be happy. One by one, the Iranian leaders passed by me and shook my hand. Some of them offered a word of kindness or gratitude, while others shook with no words at all, letting the silence do the talking. Those were the most gracious.

Reporters screamed out questions and cameramen zoomed in on my awkward smile. The older guard stood proud beside me just in case. Two other guard were pulled in behind and the three formed a triangle border between me and the outside world. After a few dozen firm handshakes, the former president stepped to me.

"Frank," said president Hallings, "What happened in there?"

The older guard broke in, "Er, sorry no questions right now, Mr. President."

"No, no. It's really okay. He needs to know now," I settled the guard. The older guard looked judgingly at the former president and nodded in slight approval.

I turned to the former president and said, "What do you want to know sir?"

The president was sweating in his speech and his nervousness was solidified when his voice seemed to crack. "Well, how did you stop the missile?"

"Ah. Something the Explosive Unit taught me. On every missile launch system there is an underlying code that stops the launch of a missile. You must set the trajectory to 360°. You see, if you set it to 0°, the missile will shoot straight up. But at 360°, the missile system understands there is a problem and refuses to launch, even though the computer will say otherwise."

The former president had no smile and no laughter. He looked shaken and sick at the same time. "Er-oh. V-very clever Frank," he managed to spit out. He began to walk away and stopped with one more flawed statement. "S-so, you showed Bernard the successful launch just before you shot him then. Yes, that is very clever."

The older guard turned a perked ear towards the former president. "Sir, I didn't mention the man's name in that building," he said with underlying suspicion, "How d-did you..." The president was struck dumb. Between two of the guards I saw the president searching for a small handgun in his pocket. Just before he drew it, *Bang!*

The former president fell to the ground dead. I had shot him.

The second I shot him, the older guard forced me to the ground and grabbed my weapon. The gun was thrown to the side and I was at the bottom of a mass of bulletproof vests and flesh. The crowd erupted again, but this time with screams and panic. The diplomats were all covered by their bodyguards and the reporters were all pushed to the dirt.

No one was standing as the former president toppled downward. The bullet wound struck him in the same spot as Bernard. The blood was already painting the dust before the old man's head hit it. I peeked out of my haven just in time to see the former president, wearing a million-dollar suit and a defeated grin, collapse dead.

I closed my eyes to the world and shielded my body. The older guard whispered somewhere in the mass, "Why'd you do that? You were safe. You were going home."

I thought about it a minute and said, "He took my home from me 17 years ago. I was just taking it back."

22

This last chapter of my novel is also the last chapter in my life. I am in a prison just outside of Washington. The crime charged against me is the assassination of former president Jeffery Hallings. When the judge called out my sentence, I didn't even flinch; I had expected this.

"Death by firing squad!" the old naïve man boomed from his stand on high.

The date was set for December 22nd. It was 8 years to the day that I had my first dream. I stood in the court room puzzling over the meaning behind such an ironic date. I found none. It was just a date. All around me, people were yelling or applauding. Some got what they wanted. Others wanted more answers.

Maybe it was the bold accusations I made against the former president that made the reporters want me alive. I revealed all secrets and composed all timelines. Still nothing changed for the jury. The truth was I had killed the former president, point blank, in front of 20 different, working cameras. There was no proof great enough for my innocence and no decision justified enough for my actions that day at the Iranian Security Council. So it was.

This prison cell is much cleaner than any room I've ever been. I don't think many people have ever stayed in this place for very long. I was brought here in a straightjacket and accompanied by three large men. They took off the straightjacket quickly before shutting the door to the rest of my life.

There isn't much light in this cell. The only light at all comes from a dull orange lamp in the corner of the hallway where the bailiff sits and takes his naps. The lamp reflects light off of the cool steel door and reflects a triangle pattern onto the floor. This is where I lie.

At night I switch to the dark side of the room and fall asleep in the corner holding onto a hard sheet of fabric. In the morning, a waffle is tossed through the bars of my door and I move back into the lighted triangle. For the rest of the day, I am buried in my thoughts.

After two days of sitting and eating and sleeping and eating, I asked the guard for a pencil and paper. After a short visit with the warden in charge of the prison, the guard came back with a red crayon and a legal pad. I thought about coloring a dinosaur for the warden, but I decided against it since I needed to finish my story first.

My first week was filled with writing in the cramped triangle of the cell with the dull crayon and yellow paper. I finished the previous chapter with anger running down my cheeks and spackling the pages with salt water. As I finished the last sentence, I was hit with the realization of my life; the purest of tragedies. I threw the legal pad against the wall and my teeth dug into my bottom lip. The guard peeked his head in to see why his only quiet patient was now a fit of rage. I looked up from my reddened eyes and asked him for a favor; a dying man's last request.

There were two things I needed from the guard; the remnants of every piece of writing I had ever created, and a lawyer. Luckily for me, both were at the same place.

Tom Long came to my cell the next morning carrying a stack of envelopes and short boxes and manila folders. When I saw him, I could tell he had matured greatly. His hair was no longer curly and left to straggle on his shoulders, but kept tight in a part across his forehead with some kind of gel. He was wearing a darker suit to hide his obviously larger body. His pants stuck out in an oval figure at the hips and he darned a rustic golden buckle across his belt. After wiping the sweat from his brow and jiggling his slacks at the waist, he embraced me with a meaningful, yet awkward hug.

"Good to see you, Frank," said Tom. I was still in a straightjacket and socks and felt sheepish next to his corporate demeanor.

"Thanks for coming, Tom."

In a whiter, rounder room, Tom and I went through the envelopes one by one. Each time I had written any part of my novel, I had sent it in some sort of packaging to Tom. Every time, I requested he not read it. I didn't care too much if he did, but when I saw the dozens of untouched parcels, I was grateful for his honor.

We went through each chapter slowly, reading aloud so both of us could take turns with our voice and both could capture the essence of the tale I was telling. After a few hours, Tom was ordered by the guard to leave and we agreed to take up the project the next day and so on after that.

To his word, Tom returned the next day with a neater pile of documents. The day after that, I noticed all of the outer packaging was shed from the paper and all that was left was delicate black folders holding the paper in place. "I'm sorry Frank, but I finished reading your story last night. I had to know."

"It's alright Tom. How'd you like it?" Tom didn't answer. He was starting to earn condensation around his eyes and he forced back his emotions before any tear could fall.

"Frank, I want to publish this novel when you die." And so we began the process of publishing my novel. The novel would not be edited except for grammar and spelling, and would consist of every piece of writing including the final chapter that I would publish the day before I die; this chapter.

For the next week, my schedule was fierce. An early wakeup was quickly followed by a two hour visit from Tom and then ended with ten hours of self reflection leading into an inevitable, harsh sleep.

Tom's visits became more and more hard to bear. With every visit came promise of the world knowing my story. But at the same time, every visit was another visit away from finding my death.

When Tom left the prison, the triangle seemed to dim even more than its already rusted tint and I became weaker. The nurses at the prison gave me regular shots of medicine to keep me from contracting a disease and spreading it to the other employees. The medicine was full of hypnotics that threw my body into a heavy numbness when I slept. I started to have dreams again. But, these weren't any dreams of purpose or relevance. They were odd and twisted and woke me into sweats of fear and panic.

The dreams would include men I knew in my platoon. They would usually be running or dying in my dreams with knives in their chests or bullet holes through their faces. Then the dream would take a sharp turn into a comedy where a dog was talking to a tree and asking if it had anymore jumbo shrimp. The entire time the tree was shaking his head defiantly, my men would still be running or still be dying in the background.

The morning, the thirty minutes I had until Tom arrived, was the only time I had to finish this chapter. So I wrote about what I knew.

In my life, there had been ironies and haphazard occurrences that neither I nor anyone could ever explain. And yet the facts remained. First, there was the path I had chosen. The small, choice steps I made throughout my existence into a dismal end. I found myself looking back over each decision I had ever made and found no right or wrong answer in any of them. They were inconsequential.

Second, I remembered Tom and Angela. How we had broken apart so early and so abruptly and now how we were thrown back together into an ill finish. Tom seemed so adult now, Angela so stunning. I had wondered if they had changed for the better and I for the worse, but couldn't get a clear answer. The only truth was that we *had* all changed and our lives were distinct because of that.

Finally, I thought about the reason I was in the cell. The assassination. The world renowned killing of former president Hallings. The video of the shooting ran through my mind like an old-time movie skipping and tearing at the gruesome parts and starting again in an equally sad position. I tried over and over to justify the action in my head.

It was just a simple reaction. It needed to be done, so you did it. Just like the train. But I was always a peaceful person. I would have lived. He could have lived. *And then what? A new Benny Angel would be born. The system would continue. You would be killed anyway. It's like the former president said, "War is inevitable, Frank."*

No, war is not inevitable, I stopped it. *Exactly. You changed the system.* But why me? There is no rhyme or reason for a death like mine. I had no hatred, no yearning for power. I was content.

That's when I realized. I had been content with the wrong things. When my parents died, I became content with being a nobody. That's when my dreams started.

They rejuvenated me. They made my life exciting. They gave me a life. After the third dream, I joined the army because that's where I *thought* I needed to be. I took orders, I killed people, and I listened to crooked power because I thought it was what I was *supposed* to do. But, it was not what I wanted.

What I wanted was a life with friends and family. A life of rhythm and decision. When I killed Bernard and President Hallings, I was ending my contentment and taking control of my life. In a way, the third dream did come true. I did save the world, just not as it was supposed to happen.

"I think you've finally figured it out, Frank." God frightened me out of my thought and stood in the dark corner of the triangle. "It took some heavy lifting to get you to this point, but I think you finally understand."

"Some of it. Will I ever understand everything?"

"In time."

"Well, I don't have much of that left, now do I?"

At this, God couldn't help but give a small laugh. He grinned at me in a way my mother would say, "It's going to be okay." Our smiles diminished in the dim cell and I questioned God one last time.

"God, the third dream, was it supposed to happen like that?"

God stood there in the shadows, a gray line hovering on his cheek. He raised a strong hand to his chin and rubbed it in deep thought. After several seconds, he turned to me and proclaimed, "You know, I'll have to get back to you on that," and he was gone. I never saw God again.

The next morning, Tom came by for one last time. He sat down on the white, rounded stool and laid a contract on the white, rounded table. This was the final contract for my novel. The work was all but done. That evening I would be handing Tom the final leaf of legal paper and begin counting the hours until my death. I offered Tom one final addition to my work. I asked him to record my final words up until my death. He would have a voice recorder with him to verify. My voice would be the last part of the novel, the period on the end of a tragic sentence.

Tom ran the idea by the warden and he said it would be perfect. Additionally, the officer had written me a note. The note explained how he had read my novel when Tom checked it through every morning and thought it was a story that needed to be told. He again documented his approval of the voice recorder and after his signature, left a post script. It thanked me for my dinosaur picture.

The last sentences of my story are being written with a heavy heart and a trembling hand. The words are formed onto the page in mistakable letters but have an unmistakable message. Tomorrow at noon, I will die.

The jostling of keys takes my eyes off of the lightning shaped crack I was staring at on the floor. I rise to my feet and peer out of my cell just as a herd of men come into the hallway towards my cell. The keys belong to the larger guard who is leading the trail for the others. Behind him is a somber priest with downward eyes and loose, grey hair.

Tucked under his arm are a floppy bible and an ancient rosary. Just to his right is the warden holding two pairs of shackles.

As the guard opens the steel door, I take one last look into my cell to see if I've forgotten anything, an old habit I learned in the army. I step out of my triangle into the full, imitation lighting that is the old lamp. The officer shackles my wrists behind my back and then my ankles. I am sifted through the hallway by the guard and we all begin our slow trek towards the shooting range.

At the end of the hallway, the silence is broken by the priest who is now shuffling his feet in unison with mine. "In the name of the father, the son, and the holy spirit," he begins. The viaticum is in earnest and deep respect. I feel the walls around me close in and become my very own shadow of death. The priest continues as we ascend into more light and finally an outside doorway.

The door is held open by the officer who offers a kind nod and last words of gratitude. From above an over hang, the sun stings my dormant eyes and I look back down towards the dirt. My feet feel soft against the coarse grain. I begin to think of running across the Arabian Desert between PT.

I am guided into position near a brick wall. My back is pushed against the wall and I feel its rigid texture. It reminds me of the train station at Foggy Bottom.

The officer unlocks my shackles and carries them away in a tangle of metal and sweat. As he walks away, he tells me that he thought I deserved to die in dignity and not tied up like a rodent. I smile and kneel down to grab a hand full of dirt. The rough powder falls through my hands like a gentle breeze and it makes me return to my baseball games and the gentle summer nights.

The priest finishes the prayer with an ordinary "Amen" and takes a seat to the side of the range. As he does this, a line of seven perfectly clad soldiers march into the opposite end of the yard. They are all my age if not younger and carry brightly polished rifles. I find a boy who looks like I did when I joined the army and I think about his innocence. I think about the innocence that I used to own, when I had Angela and Tom, and the steps I took to let it slip away.

The soldiers begin to simultaneously adorn their rifles and I begin my last set of verse. It is a hot day for a killing. The air is sticky with dew and warm breath. I feel the strength of death approaching faster now.

Cold sweat drops from my head and lands on my unshaven chin. The taste is bitter but makes me want to fight. My body wants to react with speed and power, but my mind is serene. I stand to my feet and the weight of the earth is forced onto my back. The soldiers begin their procedure.

"Ready!"

I take a last look at my hands and bite the inside of my lip. Tears fill my eyes. I steady my body into an athletic pose with my feet shoulder-width apart and my arms outstretched as if to say, "I am ready." The soldiers cock their rifles.

"Aim!"

At this command, the devilish breeze discontinues and a subtle sigh escapes my lips. My eyes travel from the ground towards my assailants, but catch an object in the corner of the range. There, tucked away after years of sun and exhaustion, is an awkward chair. The metal is rusted and the wood veneer is less than decorative, but it has a slight comfort about it. It is alone by itself in the corner with a small pack of raisins lying on its seat. I smile once to myself and I return my glare at the riflemen.

And everything goes black.

Map of Middle Eastern Landmarks

Drawing given the Warden

To the warden,

RRR

Thank for the crayons and paper